A Mid-Semester Night's Dream

A Mid-Semester Night's Dream

by

Margaret Meacham

SCHOLASTIC INC.

New York Toronto London Auckland Sydney
Mexico City New Delhi Hong Kong Buenos Aires

ISBN 0-439-85374-5

Published by Scholastic Inc., 557 Broadway, New York, NY 10012, by arrangement with Holiday House, Inc.

12 11 10 9 8 7 6 5 4 3 2 6 7 8 9 10 11/0

Printed in the U.S.A. 40

First Scholastic printing, February 2006

For my father,

James Grier Marks, Jr.

In memoriam

Chapter One

Morgan Yates was losing control of her body parts. It was all because of Ben Hennigen. That morning in seventh grade English, just before class started, Morgan's pencil rolled off her desk. Ben Hennigen jumped up, picked up her pencil, and handed it to her. For a second their fingers touched, sending a bolt of lightning through Morgan's hand, up her arm, and straight into her heart.

Since that moment, she hadn't been able to stop looking at Ben. He didn't look any different than he ever looked. He wore the same kind of

T-shirt, the same baggy pants and sneakers. His brown hair was still short on the sides and a little bit longer on top. His shoulders were broad and solid. Morgan wondered what it would be like to lay her cheek against one of those perfect shoulders.

She didn't want to be looking at Ben. She especially didn't want him to see her looking at him, but she couldn't stop. Her eyes were out of control.

Next it was her legs. At the end of the day, she was supposed to be going out the door to the school buses, but instead she found herself walking down the hall, past Ben's locker, hoping to catch a glimpse of him before she went home. Her legs were out of control.

Morgan finally got on the bus and looked for Sam Leighton, her best friend. Sam had straight, light brown hair that flopped over his forehead almost into his brown eyes. They had been friends since they were six years old, when Morgan and her dad had moved into a row house two doors down from Sam's.

Morgan remembered the day they had met perfectly. Her basset hound, Hattie, had been a puppy then, and Morgan had put her into a doll baby carriage to push her up and down the sidewalk. The wheel fell off the carriage, and Morgan was struggling to fix it when Sam came outside.

Even at age six Sam had been good at fixing things. Now he not only fixed things, but he also invented new things, too, like the ultimate alarm clock. Sam had trouble getting out of bed on time, so he made an alarm clock that first plays music, then shouts at him and flashes lights. Finally, if he's still not up, it squirts water at him. It seemed to work. Sam hadn't missed the school bus once since he'd invented his clock. Morgan was sure Sam would be famous someday.

Morgan and Sam always sat together on the bus, but rarely at school, and never at lunch. At lunch Sam sat with boys, and Morgan sat with girls, and that was usually the way it was unless you were a couple.

They would never be a couple. They were friends.

Morgan took her usual seat next to Sam, and before she could stop herself, she asked, "Did you sit with Ben Hennigen at lunch today?" First it was her eyes, then it was her legs, and now it was her mouth that was out of control.

"Yeah, why?" Sam said.

"No reason. I just wondered. Will you sit with him tomorrow?"

"I dunno," Sam said. "Why?" he asked again, this time looking at her suspiciously.

Morgan shrugged. "I just wondered." She squeezed her lips together to keep her mouth from saying anything else.

"You like him, don't you?" Sam said.

"No. Gross," Morgan said. She stared out the window at the trees and bushes bursting with their new spring leaves, not wanting Sam to see her face.

"You like him, I can tell," Sam went on.

"Shut up," Morgan mumbled.

"Ben Hennigen, huh," Sam said, smiling.

"If you say anything to him, I'll never speak to you again. Never, I swear," Morgan told him.

"I won't. Why would I?" Sam asked.

"You just better not. I mean it, Sam."

The bus stopped at the end of their street, and Sam and Morgan got off. Hattie was waiting for them inside the gate to Morgan's backyard. Morgan opened the gate, and Hattie raced out and ran in circles around them, her ears flying behind her.

Sam said, "I've got to work on Marvin. Want to help?" Marvin was the robot Sam was building for the science fair at school.

"No, thanks," Morgan told him. "I've got some stuff to do. I'll call you later."

Inside she lay on her back on the living room rug, staring up at the ceiling. Hattie lay beside her. Morgan thought about the play they were reading in English. *A Midsummer Night's Dream,* by William Shakespeare. She sighed. It was so romantic. For a minute she imagined that she was Hermia and Ben was Lysander. They would give up everything for love and leave their homes to be together, just as Hermia and Lysander planned to do. She was imagining herself wandering through the forest with Ben when the phone rang, and Morgan came back to reality with a jolt. She ran to answer the phone. It was her friend Ellen.

"Hi," Morgan said with a sigh.

"What's wrong with you?" Ellen asked.

"Nothing. I was just daydreaming," Morgan said.

As they talked, Morgan caught sight of herself in the hall mirror. No wonder Ben never noticed her. There was nothing to notice. Boring skinny figure, boring brown hair, boring brown eyes. Boring, boring, boring. And her clothes were boring, too.

"I think I need a new image," she told Ellen. "A complete makeover. I don't want to be boring Morgan anymore."

"You're not boring," Ellen said.

"The boys think I am."

"Boys. What do they know?"

"I know, but it would be nice if they knew I existed. I need to get some new clothes. Want to go to the mall on Saturday?" Morgan asked.

"Okay," Ellen said. "My mom can drop us off."

"Great. See you in school tomorrow."

Morgan hung up the phone and put on her sneakers. She would go for a bike ride. It would be the beginning of her makeover.

That night at dinner Morgan's dad said, "It's supposed to be a beautiful day Saturday. A great day for biking. We could go over to the reservoir."

"Oh, Dad, I'm really sorry, but I promised Ellen I would go to the mall with her. Do you mind if we do the biking some other time?"

"Oh. I suppose that will work. To the mall it is. What time shall we go?"

"Well, actually, Dad, Ellen and I are fine going by ourselves," Morgan told him.

"Nonsense. I don't mind taking you. You'll need a ride anyway, won't you?"

"Ellen's mom can drop us off," Morgan said.

"But I'd like to help you pick out some new things."

Morgan laughed. "Dad, there are lots of things I need your advice on, but fashion isn't one of them."

"I'm not exactly with it when it comes to style, am I?"

"Not exactly, Dad. Ellen's mom, though. Now she's a cool dresser. For a parent, I mean. And she's got great tips on makeup and stuff."

"I see. All right then. I'll leave fashion to the experts for now." Her father smiled. "Maybe we'll go biking next weekend instead."

"Right. That would be great. Dad, can I ask you something?"

"Sure, sweetie. Anything."

"Do you remember when you first met Mom?"

"Remember it? I'll never forget it."

"You were in college, right?"

"That's right. Your mom had a part-time job at the campus bookstore. I've never bought so many books in my life as I did that semester."

"What was it about her that first made you think you might, you know, like her?"

Her father thought for a minute. "Well, of course, it was everything—her eyes, her smile. But I think what really made me fall for her was the way she tilted her head."

"Tilted her head?"

"She had this way, when she was talking to you, of leaning forward a little and tilting her head, like this." Her dad put his head to one side and leaned forward. It didn't look that great. In fact he looked a little bit crazy, but Morgan figured her mom had looked a lot better when she did it. "It was as if there was nothing in the world she wanted so much as to hear what you had to say. It made me feel I could spend the rest of my life talking to her."

Morgan's mom had died in a car accident before Morgan was two years old. A lot of people thought Morgan couldn't remember her at all, but she did. She remembered her mother's soft warm arms as they carried her and her smiling face watching her lovingly.

"Everyone says I look a lot like Mom," Morgan said.

Her father nodded. "Yup. Same beautiful eyes, and same glorious smile. One of these days the boys will be falling all over themselves for a chance to talk to you."

"Oh, Dad," Morgan said, rolling her eyes. But she couldn't help smiling, too. Maybe all she needed was the head tilt. Tomorrow she'd try it on Ben.

"I've got tons of homework. I better get to it." She took her plate to the kitchen, put it in the dishwasher, and then ran up to her room.

Morgan dialed Sam's number. She heard a click as if someone had answered, and then nothing. Then she heard Sam saying, "No, you have to bring it here. Wait, no!" There was a loud crash, and Sam said, "Darn it, Marvin." Finally Sam came on the line.

"Sam? Is everything okay?" Morgan asked.

"Yeah. I'm trying to teach Marvin to answer the phone. He hasn't quite got it. He picks up okay, but he won't bring it to me."

Morgan laughed. Marvin was more trouble than he was worth. He never did anything right. "What does he do with the phone?" she asked.

"Well, just now he dropped it in the trash can, and when Ben called a while ago, he threw it out the window. I guess I have to work on his program."

"Yeah. So, Ben called?" Morgan couldn't resist asking.

"Yup."

"What'd he say?"

"Nuthin."

"Because of the phone being thrown out the window?" Morgan asked.

"No. I got the phone back," Sam said.

"Oh. He didn't say anything at all?" Morgan asked.

"Not much," Sam said. "What were you expecting him to say?"

"I just . . . thought maybe he might have said something, that's all."

"Something about what?" Sam asked.

"No one. I mean, nothing. Just forget it, Sam."

"Okay. I—Marvin, no. Those are my CDs. They're not Frisbees. I gotta go," Sam said, and the phone went dead.

Morgan tried to do her homework, but she couldn't concentrate.

A few minutes later the phone rang.

"Hi, Morgan. This is Ben. Ben Hennigen?"

"You're not funny, Sam. Not funny at all." Sam was laughing loudly as she hung up. Boys.

Morgan sighed and slammed her math book shut. Homework was so boring. She jumped up and went to the dollhouse that stood in one corner of her room. There was a spot of dirt on the roof, and Morgan rubbed it off with the sleeve of her sweatshirt. The dollhouse had belonged to Morgan's mom when she was a little girl. She had been fixing it up for Morgan when she died. Morgan loved the Victorian spires and latticework on the outside and the miniature furnishings inside.

Morgan opened the window next to the dollhouse and leaned out. The spring breeze was warm and smelled like apple trees and newly mowed grass. There was no moon, but there were lots of stars. When Morgan was little she used to look up at the stars every night, whispering her thoughts and wishes to them and believing that her mother could hear her. Sometimes she still believed it. "Are you up there, Mom?" she whispered. "I wish I could tell you about Ben. And I wish you were here to help me with my makeover."

The stars were so bright tonight. It might have been her imagination, but one star seemed to twinkle even more brightly, almost as if some-

one had heard her and was answering. Morgan took a deep breath of the fresh spring air. Things were going to work out. She would get Ben to notice her somehow. There was something about looking at the stars that made anything seem possible.

Chapter Two

The following day in English class they were discussing *A Midsummer Night's Dream.*

"Why did Lysander and Hermia agree to leave Athens and meet in the forest?" Ms. Riggs asked. "Brad? Can you tell us?"

"Um, I guess they wanted to go for a walk in the woods," Brad said.

The class giggled. Morgan and Ellen looked at each other and rolled their eyes.

Ben raised his hand, and Ms. Riggs called on him.

"They had to leave because Hermia's father

was going to make her marry Demetrius, but she really loved Lysander," Ben said.

"That's right, Ben."

"But I don't think it's fair," Ben continued. "If people really love each other, they should be allowed to get married, and Hermia's father shouldn't be able to tell them they can't."

Morgan stared at Ben and sighed.

When class was over, Morgan waited until Ben was alone and then went over to him. "I really liked what you said today," she told him.

"Thanks," Ben said.

Morgan tilted her head and leaned forward a little, just the way her father had shown her. "Do you like the play?" she asked, tilting her head a bit more.

"It's pretty good." He stared at her. "Um, are you okay?"

"Okay?"

"Your neck. Did you pull a muscle or something?"

Morgan jerked her head upright. "No, I . . . uh . . . nothing. Bye." She turned and fled. She never should have listened to her father. What did he know about love?

She didn't see Ben again until it was almost time to go home. He was coming down the hall toward her. Now was her chance. This time she wouldn't blow it by tilting her head or doing some other weird thing. She was just about to call to him when she saw Cierra Sinclair come up and tap him on the shoulder. Ben spun around. Morgan couldn't see his face, but she was sure he was smiling at Cierra. Cierra was the prettiest and the most sophisticated girl in their class. All the boys liked her.

Ben was nodding while Cierra flung her blonde hair around in that way she had. Then they walked off down the hall together. Morgan wished she had long blonde hair that she could fling around. But she wasn't Cierra. She was just boring old Morgan. Ben was never going to notice her when there were girls like Cierra around. After all, this was real life, not some fairy tale.

Later that afternoon Morgan and Sam were sitting out on the back porch at the Leightons'. Sam was working on Marvin. Hattie was scrunched up against Morgan's knees, whining. She was terrified of the robot.

"Is your mom in the kitchen?" Morgan asked. "I want to talk to her about something."

"Probably," Sam said.

Morgan went inside to find her.

Because they lived so close, and because Morgan and Sam were such good friends, the two families spent a lot of time together. Sam's parents were divorced. His dad was an engineer and lived in Colorado. Sam visited him for a month every summer, and sometimes his dad came to see him here. Morgan had met him a few times, and she liked him all right, but she really liked Sam's mother, Sally. Sally was a caterer. Her kitchen took up half the first floor of their house and was equipped with two ovens and a whole wall of freezers and refrigerators.

"Hey, girl," Sally said when she saw Morgan. "You're just in time. Try one of these. Cheese and mushroom puffs." She popped one into Morgan's mouth.

"Mmm. Yum."

"Okay, now try this one and tell me which you like best," Sally said.

Morgan tasted the second one. "Hmm. I think I like the first one best. It's cheesier."

"Good. That's my favorite, too, but I always like a second opinion. You're a much better taster than Sam. He gobbles things down so fast he hardly knows what it is. When I get around to writing my cookbook, you'll be my official taster."

Sally blew a strand of hair off her face and wiped her floury hands on a dish towel hung over her shoulder. She wore her long, honey-colored hair in a braid when she was cooking, but stray pieces were always escaping. When she was practicing new recipes at home, she wore denim overalls; but when she went out to cater, she wore a white chef's outfit.

Sally slid a tray into the oven and set the timer. "So tell me what's new."

Morgan sat on one of the stools at the counter, and Hattie sat down, too, looking expectantly at Sally.

"Oh, I know, I haven't forgotten you," Sally told Hattie. She slipped her a piece of cheese. "I don't think that will spoil her supper, will it?"

"Nothing spoils Hattie's supper," Morgan said.

Sally stroked Hattie's ears. "Is she still terrified of Marvin?"

Morgan nodded.

"I don't blame her. That robot is a menace," Sally said. "I swear it has a mind of its own."

"Sam's trying to fix him," Morgan said.

"I'll believe it when I see it." Sally pulled up a stool and sat down. "So, what's going on at school? Are you going to the dance next week?"

"I'm not sure. Do you think Sam will go?"

"He hasn't said anything, but I think he will. You should, too. It'll be fun."

"I don't know. I want to, but . . ." Morgan sighed.

Sally glanced at her. "Have you . . . thought about asking anyone?"

Morgan's face grew hot. "I've thought about it, but, I don't know. I think he likes someone else."

"You never know until you try," Sally said.

Morgan shrugged. "Yeah, but . . ."

"Is it anyone I know?" Sally asked.

"Ben Hennigen. He's a friend of Sam's," Morgan told her.

"Oh, he *is* a cutie. And nice, too. I bet he'd love it if you asked him."

"The weird thing is," Morgan went on, "I've known him for years, but all of a sudden, everything's different. It's like I never really saw him before."

Sally nodded. "I know exactly what you mean."

"You do?" Morgan asked.

"Oh yes." Sally was staring out the window, smiling.

"Sally?" Morgan said.

"Oh." Sally jumped and her face turned bright red. "I'm sorry, Morg." She began fussing with the hors d'oeuvres she was making. "Anyway, I think you should give it a try. The worst he can say is no. And you can always go single. Lots of people won't have dates."

"Yeah. I'll think about it," Morgan said.

Sally's timer went off, and Morgan saw that it was past six. "It's getting late. I better go."

"Okay, but keep me posted. Sam never tells me anything."

"I will." Morgan stood up. "Come on, Hatts."

As they went out the backdoor, Hattie cowered against Morgan; and when she saw Marvin, she raced off the porch and dashed to the back gate.

"How's it going?" Morgan asked Sam.

"He's fixed," he said, closing the panel on Marvin's chest. "I think." Sam picked up the remote control box and spoke into it. "Marvin, say good-bye to Morgan," Sam commanded.

"Bleep bleep. Bleep bleep," Marvin said. Then he bent over and picked up an apple and threw it at her.

"No, Marvin, no!" Sam cried.

Morgan laughed. "Looks like the same old Marvin to me."

Sam sighed and picked up his screwdriver.

At home Morgan went up to her room, dumped her backpack by the desk, and was about to flop down on her bed when she noticed that the front door of her dollhouse was open. That was odd. She never left the door open.

From the front, the dollhouse looked like a regular house, but the back was open, so you could reach inside and arrange the rooms. In the biggest bedroom there was a brass bedstead covered with a tiny handmade quilt and matching pillow. The children's bedrooms had toy chests and desks with real little books piled on them. There was a spiral staircase that led downstairs to an old-fashioned kitchen. When she was younger, Morgan had a family of dolls. She had spent hours playing with them in the dollhouse and making up their lives. There had been five of them—a father, a mother, and three children—the kind of family Morgan sometimes wished she had. Now the dolls were lost or broken, but Morgan still loved the dollhouse.

She looked inside and saw that the quilt on the bed in the big bedroom was thrown back, and the pillow was askew, almost as if someone had slept in it. Well, probably just the wind, she

thought. She straightened the bed and closed the door.

But later that night she saw that it had happened again. Morgan had been downstairs watching TV, and when she went back up to her room, the door of the dollhouse was open again. She was sure she had closed it firmly.

Morgan looked inside. The bed was made properly, the way Morgan had left it, but the little silver brush and comb set that normally sat on the bureau had been moved to the bathroom. It was almost as if . . . as if someone were living in the dollhouse. Morgan had once read a book about a dollhouse with dolls that had come alive. A shiver of fear ran through her.

Morgan went across the hall and knocked on the door of her father's study.

"Come in," he called.

"Dad, were you in my room just now, before I came up?" As soon as she said it, she felt dumb. Her father would never go into her room and play with her dollhouse.

But instead of denying it, he said, "Well, not

just now, no. But I . . . I was in there earlier. I—I just wanted to borrow some magazines."

"But the only magazines I have are *Teen Style* and fanzines, stuff like that. I don't think you'd be interested in them."

Then she saw that he had a stack of her magazines on his desk, and one was open to an article called "Beauty Secrets of the Stars."

"Dad? You're reading about beauty secrets?"

Her dad's ears turned red. "Um, I'm just trying to keep up, you know? I want to be able to talk to you about things that you're interested in. The way Ellen's mom does. Do you mind if I borrow them for a while?"

"Uh, no. It's fine, Dad. Be my guest," Morgan said. Her father, reading fashion magazines? She had never seen him read anything besides *The Wall Street Journal* and *Sports Illustrated,* or books about business.

"Dad, when you were getting the magazines, did you move anything around in my dollhouse?"

"The dollhouse? No, sweetie, I haven't touched it. Why? Is something missing?"

"Just some things out of place," Morgan said.

"Maybe Mrs. Keppelman moved them when she was cleaning. You can ask her when she comes on Friday."

"Right. That's probably it." Morgan yawned. "Well, I'm pooped. I'm going to bed."

"You do look tired, Morgs. You better get your beauty rest." He kissed her forehead. "Oh, and listen to this. Did you know that cucumber slices can reduce morning puffiness around the eyes?"

"No. No, I didn't know that, Dad."

"Yes. You know Serena Demuller, the actress? She uses cucumber slices all the time."

Okay, this was weird. But she couldn't hurt his feelings. "That's, uh, that's great. Thanks for the tip, Dad."

"Sure, honey," he said heartily. "Oh, if you're worried about split ends, you might try mixing an egg yolk in with a protein shampoo. Does wonders, apparently."

Morgan stared at him. "Right. Well, night, Dad."

To Morgan's relief, the phone rang and her dad picked it up. As she was leaving his study,

Morgan heard him say, "Hi, Louise. Yes. Oh, really? That's terrific."

It was that Louise Bentley. She had been calling Morgan's father a lot lately. She had come by the house last week, looking for him. Ms. Bentley had talked to Morgan as if she were a four-year-old, and had swatted Hattie away when Hattie had come up and sniffed her shoes.

Now Morgan heard her dad saying, "Saturday is perfect, Louise. It's a date. Right. See you then."

A date, Morgan thought. Reading beauty magazines and dating Louise Bentley?

This was getting serious.

Chapter Three

It was a few nights later, and Morgan had just drifted off to sleep when a noise woke her. She sat up. An eerie greenish glow came from the windows of the dollhouse. Morgan shivered. She pulled her comforter around her, took a deep breath, then climbed out of bed.

There was a loud clunk from inside the dollhouse, and then a voice said, "Oops. Oh, Hades!" Morgan froze. Then she forced herself to creep closer and peek inside.

"Hi, there. Did I wake you? I'm sorry," said the voice.

Morgan stared. A tiny person was sitting at the desk in the big bedroom, and tiny books and papers were spread out all around her. She wore jeans and a T-shirt, and there was a crown of leaves in her feathery blonde hair. A lightning bug was hovering in the air beside her, giving off the greenish light.

Morgan rubbed her eyes. She had to be seeing things. Finally she managed to sputter, "Wh-who are you?"

"I'm Gretta, of course. Gretta Fleetwing. Didn't you get the letter?"

"The letter? What letter?" Morgan asked.

"The letter from the BEF. You should have gotten it a few days ago."

"I don't know what you're talking about," Morgan said. She shook her head. This was definitely a dream.

Gretta rolled her eyes. "Well, I guess you don't if you didn't get the letter. Zeus, I can't believe it. I finally find the perfect fairy host for my humanstay, and they mess it up already."

Gretta slammed her book shut and banged her fist on the desk. The lightning bug's greenish light blinked off, then on again. "Oh, Oliver, calm down. This is Oliver," she told Morgan. "He's my pet lightning bug. And I'm telling you, he's about to make me spin my crown. He will *not* listen to a thing I say. Just goes off wherever he feels like going, and never comes when I call him. I even took him to obedience school, but it didn't do a bit of good. Of course, we only went to two classes. It was soooo boring. Honestly, I'd rather drink hemlock."

Oliver's light blinked on and off rapidly. "I know, Oliver. But we'll have to go back to obedience school if you don't listen to me." Blink blink, went Oliver.

Morgan just nodded. Tiny people didn't appear in dollhouses and start talking to their pet lightning bugs. No, they just didn't.

"Anyway," Gretta went on, "it's good to meet you, Morgan. You seem okay. Nice even. I mean, for a human." Gretta nodded. "Yes. I think you're going to be an excellent fairy host."

"Excellent what?" Morgan asked.

"Fairy host. It was all explained in the letter, but of course, you didn't get the letter."

"Umm, so how . . . how did you get here?" Morgan asked.

"I flew, of course. How else would I get here?" Behind Gretta's shoulders, a delicate pair of wings twitched. The wings were almost transparent, but at the same time they were full of a million different colors. They seemed to be still, but also in constant motion, like water in a waterfall.

"Oh. Uh-huh." Morgan nodded.

"I just don't understand why the letter hasn't come," Gretta said.

"Well, yeah, maybe my father got it, but . . ."

"No, no. It would have come to you, not him. You're the one who was selected to be a fairy host by the BEF—that's Board of Elder Fairies," Gretta explained.

"How did I get selected?" Morgan asked.

"Well, first of all you have to qualify for Fairy Assistance. You qualify under what's called the Cinderella Clause."

"What's the Cinderella Clause?"

"That's anyone who lost their mom or dad when they were very young. We're sent to advise

you about the things the mom usually clues you in on."

"They sent you to advise me?" Morgan laughed. This was some dream.

Gretta frowned. "Well, excuse me. If you don't want me to stay, I'll just pack my bags and—"

"No, no. I'm sorry. I didn't mean to laugh," Morgan said quickly.

"After all," Gretta went on, "we did get a message from the stars that you had been wishing you could talk to your mom. Of course, that can't be arranged, but we can arrange to get you the advice you need."

"Uh-huh." Morgan nodded and made sure she didn't laugh. "So . . . that twinkling star I saw a few nights ago really heard me."

"That's right. And here I am. I happen to be almost through my first year of FGTA. They don't take just anybody, you know," Gretta said.

"FGTA? What's that?" Morgan asked.

"Fairy Godmother Training Academy. After this I'll only have three more years to go."

"So you are, um, a fairy, then?" Morgan asked.

"Uh, yeaahhh. I would have thought that was pretty obvious," Gretta said.

"I thought fairies were make-believe, you know?"

"Oh yeah. I keep forgetting what you humans are like. You think all fairies should wear tutus and go around tinkling like Tinkerbell."

"Well, I just don't know that many fairies. . . ."

"Sure. I understand. This is all new to you."

"Right," Morgan said. "So, what does it mean? Being selected to be a—a what do you call it?"

"A fairy host. It just means that I'll be living with you for a few weeks, doing my humanstay. It's kind of like a field trip," the fairy explained. "We live in a human house for a while and learn the ways of humans. And we're supposed to help them if we can. Of course, we're not allowed to do real magic yet. But we can share our fairy wisdom."

"Uh-huh." Morgan nodded, but Gretta didn't exactly strike her as someone who was full of wisdom.

"Yeah," Gretta went on. "Humans are always getting themselves into such ridiculous jams. Honestly, I'm taking Human History 101 this year, and it's a hoot. You just can't help but laugh at them. Oops. I mean, no offense."

"That's okay," Morgan said. "I think history's kind of boring."

"Oh no. It's a riot. Humans are just so silly."

"Well, some are, I guess," Morgan admitted.

"Yeah. Take Helen of Troy. I mean, dating more than one guy can be okay sometimes, but you might think twice before you cause a whole war. Like, I'm all for a little harmless flirting, but there are limits."

"Well, we don't really know the whole story," Morgan said.

"And look at that French dude, Napoleon? Trying to conquer everyone just because he's got issues about his height. Talk about an ego problem!"

"Well, yeah."

"And look at George Washington. Everyone thinks he was so great, but if you ask me, the guy was a mess."

"What do you mean? He was our first president," Morgan said.

"Well, I know that. But think about it. He went around chopping down cherry trees for no good reason. He allowed them to waste all that perfectly good tea, litter up Boston Harbor. I don't know about you humans, but we fairies care about the environment."

"But—"

"And how about that old guy, Ben Franklin? He's supposed to be so smart, but even gnomes know better than to fly a kite in the middle of a thunderstorm. He's lucky he wasn't electrocuted on the spot."

Morgan wasn't sure what to say. She didn't want to offend Gretta by trying to set her straight, so she just nodded.

"By the way," Gretta went on, "this is a great place you have here." She waved at the dollhouse. "The BEF agent said it was four-star, and she was right."

"I'm glad you like it," Morgan said. "It was my mom's."

"Aww. That's sweet," Gretta said.

Morgan stood up. "I'll be right back," she told the fairy.

She tiptoed into the bathroom, turned on the light, and stared at herself in the mirror. She looked the same as ever. Same brown hair, same thin face, same wide dark eyes. She didn't look crazy. She splashed some ice cold water on her face. She pinched herself and shook her head.

Then she returned to her bedroom and sat down again beside the dollhouse. Gretta was still there, wings and all. Hattie sat down beside Morgan. "This is Hattie," Morgan told Gretta.

"I know. The BEF saw her the other day," Gretta said, eyeing Hattie warily. "She's a lot bigger than I thought she'd be. But the BEF agent said she's very gentle."

"Hattie would never hurt anyone," Morgan assured her.

"That's what they told me. She is kind of cute." Gretta held out her hand for Hattie to sniff. "Nice doggie," she said, giving Hattie a tiny pat on her nose. Then she yawned and said, "Wow. I'm beat. It's been a really long day. I was supposed to be here much earlier, but I was at Tuti's house and the time kind of got away from me. I'm sorry I woke you. I was trying to be quiet but . . ."

"That's okay. Who's Tuti?"

"Tuti's my best friend. She's a year ahead of me at FGTA." Gretta stood up and stretched. "And then I had to spend hours being debriefed by the BEF agent. She spent the night here a few nights ago, gathering data, and she needed to give me instructions."

"Oh," Morgan said. "I guess she's the one who left the door open and moved the comb and brush."

Gretta frowned. "Oh yeah. For professionals they can be incredibly careless. Honestly, you'd think they'd know better. Of course if we students screwed up like that, who knows what they'd do to us."

"It doesn't really matter. I was just curious."

"Well, I'm here now, and that's what counts, right?" Gretta said with a smile. "I guess we better go to bed before I fall asleep on my feet." She yawned again.

"Okay," Morgan said. "I have school tomorrow. Do you want to come?"

"Not tomorrow, but definitely sometime during the week," Gretta said.

"Do you need anything? Food, water?" Morgan offered.

"No, I already ate. But thanks." Gretta took off her crown and put it on the table beside the brass bed, and then turned down the comforter. "Sleep well, Morgan."

"You too. Night, Gretta."

"Oh, one more thing, Morgan. Be sure you don't tell anyone about me. That's crucial."

"Not even my friend Sam? Or Ellen?" Morgan asked.

"No one. No one else can see or hear me anyway. Only you. If you tell anyone about me, they'll just think you're crazy. Trust me, it will cause big problems for both of us. And it could get me thrown out of FGTA. I don't need any more trouble. I'm, uh"—Gretta paused—"well, I'm sort of on thin ice as it is."

"You are?"

"Kind of. It's a long story. I'll tell you all

about it tomorrow, but basically"—Gretta picked up the pillow and gave it a hard punch—"the BEF are a bunch of old farts. Honestly"—punch punch—"they *really* don't have a clue."

"Don't worry. I won't tell anyone about you," Morgan said.

"Promise?"

"I promise."

Morgan sat down on her bed. She pinched herself again until it hurt. Then she looked at Hattie. "We're awake, Hatts. This is real." She jumped up and started pacing. Back and forth, back and forth she went. "A fairy. We have a live fairy." Morgan flopped down on her chair. "Wow."

"Wowf," agreed Hattie. She sat down beside Morgan, and they both stared at the dollhouse.

Chapter Four

When her alarm went off the next morning, Morgan pressed the snooze button and was about to sleep for ten more minutes, when she remembered what had happened in the night. She sat up, ran to the dollhouse, and looked inside. There was the fairy sound asleep in the brass bed. Morgan grinned.

"Gretta?" she whispered.

"Wha?" The fairy looked up sleepily. "Oh. Hey, Morgan. What time is it? Is it morning already?"

"Yeah. I've got to go to school," Morgan said, "but I'll see you this afternoon. Okay?"

"Right. Have a good day." Gretta rolled over and went back to sleep.

Downstairs, Morgan's father was sitting at the breakfast table, drinking his coffee as usual. But this morning, instead of the newspaper, he was reading one of Morgan's fanzines.

"Hi, Dad," she said.

"Morning, Morgs."

"Was the paper boy late this morning?" Morgan asked. "Want me to check and see if the paper's here?"

"No, no. It's in my briefcase. I'll read it at the office. Hmm," he said, studying the magazine. "This is quite impressive. Brother Mother writes all his own lyrics."

"Yeah, I, uh, I heard that," Morgan said.

"And Little Meow Meow is only thirteen. Very talented for her age, isn't she?"

"I guess so, Dad." She fixed herself a bowl of cereal and sat down at the table.

"You still look kind of tired this morning, Morgs," he said. "Did the fairies keep you up last night?"

Morgan choked on her cereal. "What did you say?"

"It's just an expression, honey. It means, Did something keep you from getting a good night's sleep?"

Morgan sighed in relief. "Oh, ah, yeah, I was just sort of worried about my math test. And speaking of school, I better get going." She gave him a quick kiss and hurried out to catch the bus.

In school Morgan couldn't concentrate at all. If she wasn't thinking about Ben, she was thinking about Gretta. Morgan wanted to take good care of her, but she didn't know much about fairies. Would she be all right alone? What would she do all day? What would she eat?

As Morgan headed down the hall to her locker, she saw Ben. He smiled at her, and Morgan's heart began to pound. Her head felt light, like it might float away from her body, and her legs felt like boiled spaghetti. Keep walking. Don't stop. Don't stare, she told herself. Finally she came to her locker. She leaned gratefully against the cool metal and closed her eyes. She jumped when Ellen tapped her on the shoulder. "Hey, are you okay?"

"No. I—I mean, yes. I'm fine. It's just . . ." She sighed.

Ellen went on. "Are you going to the Mid-Semester Dance?"

"I'm not sure. I want to, but . . ."

"Yeah, I know. No date. Same with me. But we don't have to have a date. We can go with friends. Or maybe Cierra could give us some of her castoffs." She looked down the hall to where Cierra stood in a circle of boys, flinging her hair around. Morgan followed her gaze. Ben stood in the circle, a goofy smile on his lips as he watched Cierra.

"It's not fair," Morgan said.

"I know, but what are you gonna do?" Ellen asked. "There's no point in wishing for things to change."

Morgan stared at Ellen. And then it hit her. Ellen's words had given her a fantastic idea. She had a fairy living in her dollhouse. A fairy who

was in training to be a fairy godmother. Fairy godmothers could make wishes come true.

The minute she got home, Morgan rushed to her room, Hattie at her heels.

She knocked on the front door of the dollhouse. “Gretta, it’s me, Morgan,” she said, peeking in.

Gretta was sitting on the floor of the living room, leaning against the couch. There was a book open on her lap, but she didn’t seem to be reading. She was filing her nails and talking on a tiny cell phone.

“Uh-huh, uh-huh. Oh, hang on a minute, Tuti, Morgan just came home.” She took the phone away from her ear and said, “Hey, Morgan. Just a sec. Tuti’s on the phone.” She spoke into the phone again. “Look, Tuti, I better go. But I’ll call you later. Okay? You, too. Bye.” She snapped the phone shut and looked up at Morgan. “So how was school?”

Morgan knelt down in front of the dollhouse. “The same. How’s Tuti?”

"She was just calling to see how my humanstay was going. I told her it's been great so far."

"What're you reading?" Morgan asked.

"Oh, this is IFA. It's, like, one of our main textbooks." Gretta held up the book so Morgan could read the cover: *Introduction to the Fairy Arts*.

"I've got a paper I've got to work on while I'm here. Plus all the notes and reports I have to do. I'll tell you, it's a lot of work. Tuti was always complaining during her humanstay last year, but now I see what she means. I just never knew how hard FGTA was going to be."

"So what are fairy arts, exactly?" Morgan asked.

"You know, spells and charms and potions. Stuff like that," Gretta explained.

"You can do all that already?" Morgan asked.

"Not everything. Like I said, I'm just getting started in school, and I've got a long way to go. But I can do some stuff," Gretta told her.

"Cool. What type of things can you do?" Morgan asked.

"Let's see. I could turn your bed into a

pumpkin. That's one of the first things we learn. And I could probably turn Hattie into a mouse, but that's a bit trickier. I tried it one time with a chipmunk, but I messed up and turned it into a lion. I almost got eaten."

"Maybe we should leave Hattie out of it," Morgan said.

"And I can make a pretty good healing potion," Gretta went on. "Do you have a cold? This potion really helps."

"No. I'm not sick. But I wondered, do fairies ever do love charms?" Morgan asked.

"Oh yeah. We do love charms. There are, like, twenty different ones right in this book."

"Really?" Now we're getting somewhere, Morgan thought.

"Sure. Love charms are big. Of course, we haven't actually studied that yet. That's next year. Or maybe even the year after," Gretta said.

"Oh. So you couldn't, um, do one now, if someone needed one?" Morgan asked.

"We're not really supposed to practice the arts until we have a degree. But of course, *everyone* does. And I've done lots of spells that we haven't actually studied. So, yeah," Gretta nodded, "I'm sure I could do a simple love charm. Who needs one?"

"Well, actually, me." Morgan blushed.

"Oh, if it's for you I can definitely do one. I mean, I'm here to help, right?"

"Wow." Morgan smiled. "That's great."

Gretta grew serious. "We'll have to be careful, though. See, I got into a bit of trouble at my last humanstay."

"Trouble?" Morgan frowned. Maybe this wasn't such a great idea.

"It wasn't *my* fault," Gretta said quickly. "Not at all. But honestly, the BEF are just so ridiculously old-fashioned. Most of them haven't done a humanstay themselves in hundreds of years. They are *clueless* when it comes to modern humans. *So* out of touch."

"What happened?" Morgan asked.

"The main problem was that they assigned me this fairy host who was a real toadstool. This kid had, like, no friends. I mean none. I was supposed to help her make some friends."

Morgan nodded.

"Well," Gretta went on, "the minute I got there, I realized what the kid's problem was. It was just *so* obvious."

"What was it?" Morgan asked.

"It was the poor kid's mother." Gretta sighed and shook her head. "This mother would not let that girl out of her sight. Like, how is anyone supposed to make friends when their mother's hovering all over them? I had to do something."

"So what'd you do?"

"I put a simple form-change spell on the mother. Just a temporary thing," Gretta said.

"What's a form-change spell?" Morgan asked.

"All it does is change a person's form." Gretta shrugged. "I turned the mother into a parakeet. Only temporarily. It wasn't that big a deal, but the kid really got her wings in a flap." Gretta rolled her eyes. "Like I said, she was a toadstool."

"I can see how it might be pretty upsetting to have your mother turned into a parakeet," Morgan said.

"It was just supposed to be for a few hours.

To give the kid a little freedom. Some time to make friends. But it wasn't as easy as I thought. I had a bit of trouble turning her mother back into a human."

"Trouble?"

"Yeah. By mistake I turned her into a chimpanzee. But it was when I turned her into a troll that the kid really lost it. Fainted and everything. Finally I had to go to the BEF for help. I have to admit," Gretta said with a shiver, "the mom made a really ugly troll."

"But you finally got her back to a human?"

"Oh sure. Of course, the BEF weren't too happy about the whole thing. They almost kicked me out of FGTA, but my dad talked them into giving me another chance."

"That's lucky," Morgan said.

"Yeah. So this humanstay really has to work for me."

"Maybe we should just forget about the love charm," Morgan said. She didn't want to get Gretta into trouble, and she really didn't want to be turned into a troll.

"No, no, no." Gretta waved away Morgan's

doubts. “This is a different situation entirely. First of all, there’s nothing easier than love charms. Everyone does them. And nothing can go wrong. They’re gnome-proof. Trust me.”

“You’re sure?”

“Absolutely.” Gretta nodded decisively. “So,” she said, folding her hands on top of her book and looking at Morgan, “tell me about the LO.”

“LO?” Morgan asked.

“Love object. Is he cute? What’s his name?”

“Ben Hennigen,” Morgan said. “And he’s really cute. At least I think he is.”

“Uh-huh.” Gretta went back to filing her nails. “Does he go to your school?”

“Yes. And see, there’s this dance next weekend, the Mid-Semester Dance?”

“And you want to go with him?” Gretta said.

“Right. But I get so nervous every time I’m near him. I’ll never be able to ask him.” Morgan started pacing.

“Well, that sounds simple enough.” Gretta opened her fairy arts manual and began flipping through it. In a minute she said, “Okay. Here we go. LC six—a simple but effective love charm.”

"Umm, how does it work, exactly?" Morgan asked. She paced faster.

"Hmm. Let's see." Gretta read through the love charm, nodding her head. "Okay, okay. Would you slow down, Morgan? You're making me nervous. This is as easy as mudpies." She read the ingredients. "'Fourteen grains of fairy dust.' I've got that." She pulled out a little bag and rummaged through it. "'Wand.' I've got that. 'Chalk.' Can you get some chalk?" she asked.

"Sure. I've got some chalk around here somewhere," Morgan said, rummaging through her desk.

"Okay, then." Gretta snapped the book shut and smiled. "We're all set."

"What will happen?" Morgan asked, then bit her lip. "What if something goes wrong?"

"Would you please trust me? You humans have no respect for our talents. All that will happen is that the LO will find you irresistible," Gretta explained.

"So if I ask him to go to the Mid-Semester Dance with me, he'll say yes?"

"Absolutely."

Morgan thought for a minute, then took a deep breath. Gretta seemed very sure about this. And Gretta didn't want to get into trouble, either. She wouldn't do it if anything could go wrong. "Okay. Let's go for it."

"Great!" Gretta said. "But this particular love charm works best after sunset. We'll have to wait awhile."

"My dad will be home soon. We can do it after he goes to sleep."

"Okay. And in the meantime, I'll read over the charm and brush up on the incantation."

"I guess I better start my homework." Morgan stood up and went to her desk. Then she went back to the dollhouse. "But, I wondered, are you hungry? I'm not sure what fairies eat, but I could get you something."

"Oh, hey, thanks, but I went down to the kitchen after I heard everyone go out and helped myself. Fairies eat pretty much the same things as humans. You might bring me a bit of dinner later, though."

“Okay, sure.” Morgan smiled. By this time tomorrow, Ben would find her irresistible.

Morgan was doing her homework when she heard her father’s car pull up. Through the window she saw him park. Someone was with him. Morgan leaned forward to get a better look.

“What is *she* doing here?” Morgan said.

“Who?” Gretta asked. She was sitting on the steps of the dollhouse reading her IFA.

“Louise Bentley. She’s this creepy woman that my dad’s been hanging out with lately.”

Gretta put her book down and flew over to the window. “You mean, like, dating her?”

“Well, he had a date with her last Saturday while I was at the mall with Ellen, and now here she is again.” As Morgan and Gretta watched, Morgan’s dad and Ms. Bentley came up the front walk and into the house.

“She does look kind of creepy. That hair is so yesterday. But I could see how your dad might think she’s pretty,” Gretta said.

“Ugh. I hope not,” Morgan said. “She better not be staying for dinner.”

"Morgan?" her dad called. "Would you come down here for a minute, honey?"

"I'm in the middle of homework, Dad," Morgan called.

"I just want you to say hello to someone."

Morgan looked at Gretta and pretended to gag, but she got up from her desk and went downstairs. Her father and Ms. Bentley were sitting in the kitchen. "Morgan, dear! There you are. Don't you look precious," Ms. Bentley said.

"You remember Ms. Bentley, don't you, Morgs?"

Morgan nodded. "Hello," she said.

Hattie had followed Morgan into the kitchen. She wagged her tail and put her paw up for Morgan's dad to take. "Yes, I'm glad to see you, too, Hattie," he said, patting her. But when Hattie turned toward Ms. Bentley, the woman jumped up and headed for the door. "Well, I'd better run. I don't want to keep our industrious little student from her homework. I'll call you tomorrow, Jim. And maybe we can get together on Friday."

Her dad followed Ms. Bentley out to the front steps and they talked for another few minutes.

"Don't let her bother you, Hatts," Morgan said as they went back upstairs. "She's not worth it."

That night at dinner, Morgan's father said, "So how was your day? Anything new in your life?"

If he only knew, Morgan thought and grinned. "Well, there's a dance coming up at school," she said. "The Mid-Semester Dance."

"Great!" he said. "I guess you'll be going?"

"I'm not sure yet."

Her father folded and unfolded his napkin over and over again. "Uh, I guess some of your friends are starting to think about boys?"

"Yeah."

"Mmmmm. And of course, that's very normal at your age. At any age. I mean, any age over a certain age, if you know what I mean," he said.

"Right, Dad."

"Maybe you'd like to get a new dress to wear?"

"I would like a new outfit," Morgan said.

"Great. We'll go shopping sometime next week," he said.

"Dad, you hate shopping for clothes," Morgan said, smiling and leaning over to give him a peck on the cheek.

"But this is a big occasion. Your first real dance. We could look through those fashion magazines tonight and see what—"

"I've got tons of homework tonight, Dad. But it would be great if we could go shopping before the dance."

"Wonderful. I'll come home early one day, and we'll shop till we drop!" he said.

"Good." Morgan finished her dinner. "That was the best potato salad. Did you get it at Eddie's?"

"Sally gave it to us. Left over from a barbecue she catered. It is good, isn't it?"

"Sally's the best cook," she said.

"I'll say," he agreed.

Morgan stood up and began clearing their plates.

"I've got some phone calls to make," her father said. He took the portable phone out onto the deck, and Morgan heard him talking quietly.

She peeked out the window and saw him laughing. It didn't look like a business call. She hoped it wasn't Louise Bentley.

Morgan quickly took a little plate out of her pocket. It was actually the top of a small round china box that she kept on her bureau, just the right size for Gretta. Morgan cut off a morsel of the leftover hamburger and a pinch of bun, and made Gretta a tiny burger. She put a bit of potato salad on the plate, and cut a string bean into pieces. Then she took an apple, cut off a small slice, and cut it up. Perfect.

She took the plate upstairs and knocked on the dollhouse door.

"Yo. Come on in," Gretta called. "Oh, wow, a feast," she said when she saw the plate of food. "Thanks, Morgan. So"—she took a bite of the hamburger—"tell me about Ben."

"Well, he's in my English class." Morgan sat down next to the dollhouse and told Gretta about what he had said about *A Midsummer Night's Dream*.

"Wow. He sounds pretty enlightened. For a guy."

They talked some more until Gretta finished her dinner and patted her stomach. "That was delicious. I'm so full I could pop. Now I'll prepare the love charm, and as soon as everything quiets down we'll get to work."

Later that night, when she was sure her dad was sound asleep, Morgan tiptoed back to the dollhouse.

"Is it time?" she whispered.

"All set." Gretta grabbed her wand and flew out into the middle of the room. "Okay. You've got the chalk?"

Morgan nodded.

"Now," Gretta said, "draw a circle in the middle of the rug here. Big enough for you to kneel inside."

Morgan took the chalk and traced a circle on her green rug, then knelt inside. "Now what?" she asked.

Gretta flipped through her manual to the proper page. "Here we go. All you have to do is close your eyes and picture the LO—that would be Ben—in your mind. Just do that. I'll do all the rest."

Morgan closed her eyes and pictured Ben. "I feel kind of dumb," she said.

"You won't feel dumb tomorrow when he flips his crown over you." Gretta took her wand and flew around the circle three times. Then she chanted a string of words that sounded like a foreign language. She sprinkled some dust and waved her wand over Morgan and said some more words. Finally she said, "Okay. All done. Tomorrow Ben will find you irresistible. He won't be able to say no to you."

"But I don't feel any different." Morgan stood up. "Do I look different?"

"You're not supposed to feel any different. Or look different," Gretta told her. "He won't feel different, either. He'll just notice you all of a sudden, and want to be with you."

"Perfect. Oh, thank you, Gretta. I can't wait until I see him." Morgan spun around, laughing.

But Gretta was studying the spell book, her brow furrowed. "Oops."

"What? Is something wrong?" Morgan asked.

Gretta slammed the book shut and smiled at Morgan. "Don't get your wings in a flap. By tomorrow night you'll have a date for the Mid-Semester Dance. I can almost guarantee it."

Morgan felt a twinge of doubt. "Almost? I thought you said it was a sure thing."

"Well, nothing is ever certain. Surely even humans know that."

Chapter Five

Morgan was putting her books into her locker when she saw Ben coming down the hall. This was it. For the first time she felt almost calm, not scared and nervous the way she usually felt when he was around.

He stopped at his locker and began pulling books out of his backpack. Morgan took a deep breath and flung her hair back the way she had seen Cierra do. She walked up right behind him and was just about to say hi, when her nose began to tickle. All that came out was, "Ahh-ahhhh-AHHHHHHHCHOOOOOO!"

Ben jumped. "Oh," he said when he saw her. "Bless you."

Morgan sneezed again.

"Bless you again," Ben said.

She sneezed again.

"Umm," Ben said.

She kept sneezing. Her sneezes got louder and louder.

Ben stared.

This was not supposed to happen. She couldn't talk; she couldn't move. All she could do was sneeze.

"Are you okay?" Ben asked. He backed away from her, pressing up against his locker.

She shook her head and with one final blast dashed away to the girls' restroom.

In the mirror she saw her eyes were red and puffy, and her nose was running. She looked like a squashed tomato.

"Hey, what happened to you?" Ellen asked, walking in.

"I had a sneezing fit," Morgan told her. "I couldn't stop."

"You must have a really bad cold. Do you feel awful?" she asked.

"No. I don't think I have a cold. I feel fine. But it wasn't just ordinary sneezing."

"You must be allergic to something. Allergies can cause spells like that," Ellen said.

"Spells?" Morgan's eyes widened.

"Sneezing spells. I've got to get to class. Hope you feel better."

Morgan slapped her forehead and moaned. Gretta! Gretta had messed up the spell. Instead of making Morgan irresistible, she had made her sneeze. But Morgan only sneezed when Ben was around, and the only class she had with him was computer lab at the end of the day. If she could avoid him all day, and then make sure to sit across the room from him in computer lab, maybe it would be okay. Then when she got home she would get Gretta to straighten things out.

Morgan left the bathroom and ran into Sam.

"Hi. How's your cold? Ellen said you had a sneezing fit," he said.

"It's better," Morgan said.

"Good. I've got some great news for you. I did you one huge favor." Sam grinned.

"Oh yeah? What?" Morgan asked.

"You know how we've got computer lab this afternoon?"

"Yeah?"

"Well guess who I was assigned as a lab partner? And guess who I switched with?" Sam said.

"Wh-who?" Morgan said faintly, leaning against a locker for support. She had a sinking feeling she already knew the answer.

"Ben Hennigen. And you! You're lab partners! Isn't that fantastic?"

"Oh, no. No. That's terrible." Morgan grabbed Sam's sleeve. "I can't be his lab partner. You've got to switch back with me."

"But why, Morgan? Could you calm down and let go of my shirt? Look, I know you like him. You can be honest. I won't say anything to him. And it's the perfect chance for him to notice you. Isn't that what you want?"

"No, Sam, you don't understand. You've got to switch back."

"Morgan, I can't switch back. Mr. Sweeney's already written up the lab partners. It's too late."

Morgan started pacing and muttering. "I can't go. That's all. I won't go to lab today."

Sam laughed. "That'll go over well with Sweeney. You know how nuts he is about us missing lab. If he finds out you were in school and didn't go to lab, do you know what he'll do to you?"

"It's true." Morgan sighed. "He's a fanatic about labs."

"Look, Morgan, I don't get it. I thought you'd be happy," Sam said.

"I know it seems crazy to you. Just trust me. I can't sit next to him." Morgan moaned, "Oh, what am I gonna do?"

When Morgan walked into the lab, she sat as far away from Ben as she could get. Maybe they wouldn't have to work with their partners right away. Sometimes Mr. Sweeney lectured before they did their projects. Maybe today they wouldn't have to work together at all. Maybe there would be a lecture, a fire drill, something—anything.

Mr. Sweeney came into the classroom. "Okay, class, we'll get right to work. Partners, please get together. If you don't know who your partner is, check the list."

Ben got up and checked the list. He looked across the room at Morgan and smiled. Her heart did that flip that it did every time she looked at him. Please, please let the spell be gone, she prayed.

He got his books and came over to the empty seat next to hers. "Hi. How's your cold?" he asked.

"It's . . . better," Morgan said. So far, so good. But then she felt it. The tickle. She was not going to sneeze. She clamped her mouth shut. She held her breath. She would not sneeze. She would not—**"AHCHOO!"** Morgan erupted.

"Now class, today we have an important project to work on. Please boot up your computers and—"

"Choo!" She couldn't stop. **"AHCHOO AHCHOO AHCHOO!"** She sounded like a car alarm.

She glanced at Ben. He looked worried.

“**AHCHOO!**” went Morgan. It was the loudest one yet. People started laughing, and Mr. Sweeney looked over at her, annoyed.

“**AHCHOO!**”

The whole class was laughing now, except for Morgan and Ben and Mr. Sweeney.

“Are you all right?” Ben whispered.

“No. **AHCHOO.**”

Sam was staring at her, his mouth wide open.

“Ms. Yates,” Mr. Sweeney said, “would you like to be excused? Perhaps you should see the nurse.”

Morgan nodded, and still sneezing she fled the classroom.

Behind her the computer lab exploded in laughter.

Mrs. Grossinger, Morgan's science teacher, was marching down the hall as Morgan stepped out of the classroom. She was one of the strictest teachers in the school, and she carried a ruler at all times. She believed in discipline with a capital D.

"Gracious heavens." Mrs. Grossinger frowned disapprovingly when she heard the laughter from the classroom. "What's going on in there?" She glared at Morgan. "And why are you in the hall instead of in class?"

"I—I'm not feeling well, Mrs. Grossinger. I'm going to the nurse's office."

"Be on your way then." Mrs. Grossinger waved her ruler at her. "No loitering in the halls."

"Yes, Mrs. Grossinger," Morgan said. Her sneezing had stopped.

Chapter Six

"What happened to you?" Sam asked when Morgan collapsed into her seat on the bus. "I've never heard anything like that before."

"I don't want to talk about it, okay?" Morgan leaned her forehead against the window.

"Yeah, okay, but man, those were some industrial-strength sneezes. I didn't know anyone could—"

"Sam! I said I don't want to talk about it."

"Okay, okay." He was quiet for a few minutes. Then he said, "Are you going to the dance on Friday?"

"I haven't decided."

"Would you go if Ben was going?" Sam asked.

"Maybe. But he thinks I'm a freak after the way I sneezed."

"No, he doesn't. He thinks it's cool that you got out of lab. He said he wished he could sneeze like that. Then he'd never have to sit through Mr. Sweeney's lectures."

"Really?" Morgan said.

"Yup. So are you going?" Sam asked.

"I don't know. Is Ben going?" Morgan asked.

"He doesn't know. I bet he'd go if you were going," Sam told her.

"But how will he know if I'm going?" Morgan asked.

"I could tell him," Sam said.

"Would you?" Morgan asked.

"I could," Sam said.

"Would you go if Ellen was going?" Morgan asked. She was pretty sure Sam liked Ellen.

"Is she going?" Sam asked.

"I don't know. But I could find out." Morgan smiled.

"Could you tell her I'll go if she goes?"

"I could," Morgan said.

"Shake," Sam said, sticking out his hand.

They shook.

Now all Morgan had to do was get rid of the spell.

"Gretta!" Morgan pounded on the door of the dollhouse. Gretta was sitting sideways in one of the living room armchairs, her legs slung over one arm. She was on the phone again. "You're joking. She really said that?" She held up a finger, signaling for Morgan to wait a minute.

Morgan fumed. "I need to talk to you now, Gretta."

"Let me call you back, Tuti," Gretta said. She hung up and looked at Morgan.

"Hey, girl. What's up?"

"Sneezes, that's what's up," Morgan cried. "What did you do to me?"

"What're you talking about?" Gretta asked.

"The spell. It made me sneeze the minute I got near Ben. The loudest sneezes ever. I've never been so embarrassed in my whole life."

"Uh-oh. Did we blow it?"

"We? We didn't blow it. You blew it." Morgan flopped down on the floor. "It was awful. These were not ordinary sneezes. We're talking industrial strength here. It was horrible."

"Crickets, I'm really sorry, Morgan. But I can fix it. I know I can. See, what happened was, I just got a little of the incantation wrong. I didn't think it would matter, but I guess it did." She thought for a minute. "I know. I'll talk to Tuti. She had Intro to Love Charms last semester. She can tell me what to do."

"Just get rid of the spell," Morgan said. "I can't go around sneezing every time I see Ben. Either you get rid of it or I'm going to have to move to a new town."

"Okay, okay. Keep your crown on. I'm calling Tuti right now. She always knows what to do."

While Gretta dialed her cell phone, Morgan's own phone rang. It's probably Sam, she thought, and she ran to answer it.

"Hello?" she said.

"Hello. Is this Morgan?" It wasn't Sam.

"Yes, this is Morgan."

"Hello, dear! How are you? This is Ms. Bentley. Remember me?" She spoke slowly, as if Morgan were two years old.

"Yes, I remember you, Ms. Bentley."

"Good, dear. Now I wonder if you can help me. I'm looking for your daddy. Would he be available?"

"He's not home from work yet," Morgan told her.

"Oh. I tried to get him at the office, but he's not there, either. Ask him to call me when he gets home. Do you think you can remember to do that, dear?"

"Yes," Morgan said. "Can I have your number?"

"Oh, he has my number. Now don't forget. All right, Morgan? Bye now."

Morgan hung up and went back to her room. "Grrr. That woman is stalking my father," she told Gretta. But the fairy was still on the phone. She was nodding and writing notes on a tiny piece of paper.

"Okay. Mmmmm. Right. Right. Let me check, hold on." Gretta rummaged in her backpack and

found a little tube. "Tincture of Bees' Wings," she read. She picked up the phone again and said, "Yup. I've got some." She listened, nodding for a while, and finally said, "Okay, great. Thanks, Tuti. Talk to you later."

She hung up and said to Morgan, "We're all set. Tuti knows all about love charms. See, this Tincture of Bees' Wings erases the spell. All I have to do is rub it on your palms, and say the incantation. Next time you see Ben, you'll be totally back to normal. We'll do it tonight right before you go to bed. By tomorrow, no more sneezes," Gretta told her.

Morgan raised her eyebrows. "You're sure about this?"

"Trust me. It's as simple as mudpies."

Chapter Seven

The next morning Morgan stumbled into the bathroom with her eyes half closed. She splashed her face with water, looked at herself in the mirror, and screamed. It was a loud, piercing scream that shook the pipes and rattled the windows.

"Oh no," Morgan whispered. "What has she done to me?"

Her father came running. Quickly Morgan locked the bathroom door. "Morgan! What is it, honey? What's wrong?"

"I'm—um—I'm sorry, Dad. N-nothing's wrong. I was just—um—practicing."

“Practicing? Practicing what?” her father asked from the other side of the door.

“Practicing my scream. Um—in case something is wrong sometime.” Morgan shut her eyes tight and gripped the counter.

“Morgan, you scared me half to death. This is not the way I like to wake up.”

“I—I’m really sorry, Dad. I didn’t know it would be so loud.”

“Next time you practice screaming, do it quietly, all right?”

“Right, Dad.”

His footsteps thumped away, and Morgan peeked at herself again. Then she stared. She was blue. Her face, her hands, her chest, her stomach, every bit of skin she had was a bright royal blue. Blue like a character in a Dr. Seuss book. Blue like a Smurf. Morgan grabbed the soap and began to scrub, but nothing happened. She was still blue.

Morgan unlocked the bathroom door, checked to make sure her father’s bedroom door was closed, and crept back into her own room, locking the door behind her. "Gretta," she whispered. "Gretta, wake up. Now!"

"Morgan? Hey, what time"—Gretta opened one eye and caught sight of Morgan—"uh-oh."

"Uh-oh is right. Look at me," Morgan cried. "You've got to do something."

"Look, don't panic. Just . . . just calm down."

"Don't panic? You turn me blue and then you tell me not to panic? Do you think I want to be blue? Do you think I like being blue?" Morgan stomped her foot.

"Don't get your wings in a flap. It's not permanent. It'll wear off."

Now she was pacing. "When? Half an hour? I have to be at school in an hour. It better be gone by then."

"Well, it might take a little longer than that," Gretta mumbled.

"Like how much longer?"

"Maybe about a day."

"A day?" Morgan flopped onto her bed and pulled a pillow over her head.

"About that."

"Look, Gretta." Morgan took a deep breath and tried to speak calmly. "I have a huge history test tomorrow. Today is the final review. I cannot miss it. I have to go to school, and I cannot go to school if I am blue. You turned me blue, now you better turn me back. Do you understand?"

Morgan's father knocked on the door.

Morgan sat up. "Um, don't come in, Dad. I'm dressing."

"I just want to tell you that I have to leave early. I'll see you this evening, okay?"

"Okay, Dad."

"Morgs?" he said. "Are you all right? You sound kind of blue."

"Blue? I—I'm not blue, Dad. No. I'm not blue at all," she called to him. Then she muttered, "If he only knew."

"You're not upset about something?" he asked.

"No. I'm fine, Dad," Morgan said. She glared at Gretta and mumbled, "Just tickled pink."

"All right then, sweetie. Have a good day."

"You too, Dad." She heard him running

down the stairs. "Phew. Lucky he has to leave early. At least I won't have to worry about giving him a heart attack when he sees me."

Gretta held up the tube of Tincture of Bees' Wings. "See, the problem is the tincture's expired. I saw the date on the tube, but by then it was too late. I was hoping it wouldn't matter, but I guess it did."

"I guess so," Morgan said bitterly.

"Well, crickets, it's not the end of the kingdom. It's just one day. And it is a pretty color. You've been talking about how you want a makeover."

Morgan glared at her.

"Just kidding," Gretta said, laughing.

"You think this is funny?" Morgan cried.

"Look," Gretta said. "I'll do a form-change spell on you. I'll turn you into a mouse or a parakeet. Then you can go—"

"No!" Morgan shouted. "No more spells!" She collapsed on her bed again. Hattie jumped up beside her and gave her a paw to hold. "What am I gonna do, Hattie? Too bad I don't have a fur coat like you."

"Hey, that's an idea," Gretta said, and whirred around the room excitedly. "All you have to do is cover yourself up. Pretend it's a costume."

"A costume? Halloween was months ago." Morgan thought for a minute. "I could wear tights and a long-sleeved shirt and gloves, but what about my face?"

"A mask."

"Why would I wear a mask to school?"

"You're in a play?"

"I'm not, and even if I were, you don't wear your costume all day."

"You could say it's an experiment. You want to know what it's like to . . . to be faceless or something."

"Hmm." Morgan stared at her values textbook sitting open on her desk. Last week they had read an article called "Our Image-Conscious Culture." It was all about how television and advertising make people value the way a person looks instead of the way they act and what they're like inside. Morgan had agreed with the article. "A protest, maybe."

"A protest?" Gretta hovered over Morgan's bed.

"Yes. I could wear a ski mask. I could say I'm protesting our image-conscious culture."

Gretta clapped her hands. "That's brilliant. That'll work for sure."

Morgan pulled out a bin from her closet that held her ski stuff and found a black knit ski mask that covered everything but her eyes and her lips. She dressed in black jeans, a white turtleneck, gloves, and the ski mask. When she was done, not one inch of her blue skin showed.

On the school bus she took her usual place next to Sam.

"Morgan?" he said.

"Yup."

"What's with the ski mask?"

"It's a protest."

"Against what?"

"Our image-conscious culture."

"Oh. That's cool." But he kept on staring at her.

"What?" she asked.

"Nothing, it's just . . . this isn't about your hair again, is it?"

"My hair? What're you talking about?"

"Remember last summer when you hated your haircut and you wore that weird hat all the time?"

"This is nothing like that. This doesn't have anything to do with my hair." That much was true. Her hair was the only part of her that wasn't blue. "And anyway, I liked that hat."

"Whatever," Sam said. "You think they'll let you wear that in school?"

"Of course. Peaceful protests are a constitutional right," Morgan told him.

Sam nodded. "I don't think Mrs. Grossinger believes in constitutional rights."

Sam was right. The minute Mrs. Grossinger saw Morgan, she stopped her and asked, "Is that you, Morgan? Why are you wearing that mask? Take it off immediately."

"But—but I can't, Mrs. Grossinger. It's, uh—" She wouldn't even try to tell Mrs. Grossinger about her protest. It'd never work.

"What if everyone decided to wear a mask to school? What then?" Mrs. Grossinger snapped

her ruler. "Chaos, that's what. And that's exactly why we have rules about matters such as this."

"But I can't take it off. Really I can't. It's, uh, it's a medical condition."

"I see. I assume, then, that you have a note from your doctor?"

"I forgot to bring one. But—I could have my doctor call you."

"All right. You may wear the mask, but I'll expect to hear from your doctor by the end of the day. What is his name?"

"His name? His name is . . . well, actually it's not a him; it's a her. Her name is Dr. Fleetwing. Dr. Gretta Fleetwing."

"You told her what?" Gretta cried.

"Look, it's not like I had a choice. It was that or take the mask off. Can you imagine what would have happened if they'd seen this?" Morgan pointed to her face, which was still blue, though not as bright as it had been earlier. "Talk about chaos."

Gretta crossed her arms and beat her wings furiously. "I just don't know why you had to involve me in this. If the BEF find out I've impersonated a doctor—"

"Involve you? Are you joking? You're the one who got me into this mess. And anyway, the BEF won't find out. All you have to do is make a simple phone call."

"All right, all right, I'll do it. But first I have to remove my silencer with an anti-silence spell. That way she'll be able to hear me." Gretta opened her IFA, read a spell, and sprinkled fairy dust over herself. "There. All set. Actually, this might be kind of fun. I'm pretty good at impersonations. Yes. I think I know just the accent to use."

"That's fine. But we've got to hurry. Do you want to use your cell phone?"

"I can't call humans on my cell phone. It's the Spider One Network. Only fairies can be connected."

"Well, we'll have to use my phone then. Come on. Sit there on the bed, and I'll hold it for you."

Morgan knelt beside the bed and dialed the number Mrs. Grossinger had given her. Then she held the phone so that Gretta could talk into it, while Morgan listened.

"Honoria Grossinger here." Mrs. Grossinger's voice came on the line.

Gretta sat up and spoke into the mouthpiece of the phone. "Allo. Zeez eez Doctor Fleetwing. I am calling about a student een your school. Her name eez Morgan Yates."

"Yes, Doctor. Thank you for calling. Morgan claims to have a medical condition that requires her to wear a ski mask to school."

"Zese eez corrhect. I haf told her to wear zee mask."

"This seems very unusual to me, Doctor."

"Yess. It eez an unusual condeetion. A skeen condeetion. Zee mask prevents contagion."

"Oh my. If it's contagious Morgan will have to stay at home. We can't risk infecting other students."

"No, no. Zee condition will be gone by tomorrow. I haf prescribed a potion."

"A potion?"

Morgan shook her head frantically. "A medicine," she whispered to Gretta.

"I meen to say a mediceen," Gretta said. "A

potent mediceen. Zee condition will be gone by tomorrow. Now I must be gone. I haf many other patients to feex."

Morgan hung up the phone. "Whew. That was great. I think she bought it."

"Totally."

"So tell me, Dr. Fleetwing. Will my condition really be gone by tomorrow?"

Gretta nodded. "Absolutely. You look better already."

Morgan looked at herself in the mirror. "It's fading, but it's still blue. Yikes. Here comes Dad." She pulled the ski mask back on and found her gloves. In a minute her father called from downstairs.

"Hi, Dad. I'm in my room."

He came upstairs and stopped at her door. "Hi, sweetie. What's with the mask and gloves?"

"It's, um, a new beauty treatment. I read about it in one of my magazines. Wearing a mask after you apply moisturizer helps you absorb it better. Same thing with the hands."

"I've never heard that, but it sure sounds

logical. Listen, hon. Sally said she has lots of left-overs from an event she catered last night, so we're going over there for dinner. Okay?"

"Sorry, Dad. I've got tons of homework." Normally she loved it when they ate at the Leightons', but she couldn't go over there wearing her ski mask.

"Well, I'm going over now, but we probably won't eat for a while, so you can work on your homework now."

When he was gone Morgan said, "Great. Just great. Now I'm going to have to call and say I'm sick or something. I'll miss dinner and probably starve to death, and I still haven't asked Ben to the dance."

Gretta was sitting on the steps of the doll-house, filing her nails. "Well, there is something we haven't tried yet. Something that works every time."

"Not another spell?"

"Well, yes, but this one really is gnome-proof."

Morgan threw up her hands. "After what I've been through, do you really think I'd want to try another spell? Do you think I'm insane?"

"Look, I know the first two tries didn't work out so well. But this one is a sure thing. Trust me."

"That's what you said last time." Morgan flopped down on her bed. She was beginning to wish she'd never heard of the Mid-Semester Dance.

Gretta flew over and perched on the edge of her bedside table. "It's a naming spell. Everyone knows that naming spells are the easiest kind to do."

"So why didn't you do that one to begin with?" Morgan asked.

"Because to do a naming spell I have to come to school with you." Gretta opened her IFA and began flipping through it. "Look. It's right here. Listen to this. 'Highly recommended. When the parties are in close proximity, the spell is most effective.'"

"What does that mean?"

"See, I come to school with you, and when we see Ben I sprinkle some fairy dust on him, say the incantation, and then the next person who says his name is the person he falls in love with."

"So all I have to do is say his name?" Morgan asked.

"Right. What could be easier?"

"I don't know. . . ."

"Listen. I know I screwed up on the first two, and I feel really bad about it," Gretta said. "Just give me one more chance. I really want to make it up to you."

Morgan flipped over on her stomach and looked at the fairy. Gretta looked sincere.

"Besides," Gretta went on, "I have a good feeling about you and Ben. I think you two were meant to be together."

"You really think so?" Morgan smiled.

"I do. We fairies have ways of knowing these things."

"Well, I guess we could try one more time," Morgan said.

"That's the spirit," Gretta said, clapping her hands. "This time we'll get it right, and in a few days you'll be dancing with Ben at the Mid-Semester Dance."

Chapter Eight

"No one but me will be able to see you, right?" Morgan asked as she walked to school with Gretta riding on her shoulder. She had decided to walk rather than take the bus so that she could talk to Gretta. It was a bright sunny day, and Morgan was glad to be outside in the warm spring air.

"Right. No one but you."

"And you're sure the spell will work this time?"

Gretta glared at Morgan. "If you ask me that one more time, I'm going to put a silencing spell on you."

"Okay, okay. You can't blame me for being worried after the last two disasters, can you?" Morgan said.

"I thought I explained all that," Gretta said.

"Look, we probably won't see Ben until later, so you'll just have to come with me to class this morning. No one can hear you, either, can they?"

"No one but you."

"But I won't be able to talk to you once we're at school, or people will think I'm crazy. Just remember that, okay?"

"Righto. This should be interesting. I've never been to a human school before. Are your classes in a meadow or a grove?"

"Huh?"

"Most of our classes are in a meadow, but on hot days they're in a shady grove," Gretta said.

"Ours are inside. In classrooms. We're humans, not fairies."

"Oh, right."

"Yeah, and it's a big school. It can be pretty confusing, so stay with me."

"Sure." Gretta looked over her shoulder. "Uh-oh."

"What?"

"Look who's here. He must have followed us. Oliver, I told you to wait for me at home."

The lightning bug flew in front of them and blinked his light on and off several times.

Gretta shook her head. "Well, I guess you can come. But you can't cause any trouble. Just stay with me and Morgan, all right?"

He blinked again and settled on Gretta's shoulder.

"Don't worry," Gretta told Morgan. "I made him invisible to everyone but you."

They were close to school now, and Morgan saw some kids she knew. "Look, I can't talk any-more now," she whispered. "My first period is science. It's pretty boring, and Mrs. Grossinger is my strictest teacher."

They went into the school building and came to the lockers, where Morgan unloaded her books. She waited until the bell rang, hop-ing to see Ben, but he wasn't around, so she hur-ried down the hall to science.

As soon as they entered the classroom, Gretta screamed.

"What? What's wrong?" Morgan whispered.

"That board." Gretta pointed to the specimen board with a shaking hand. "With those poor butterflies. And beetles. Look at them stuck there like that. It's horrible."

"They're just dead bugs," Morgan whispered.

"Poor Oliver. This could traumatize him," Gretta said. Oliver blinked rapidly and flew in circles around Gretta's head. "It's okay, Oliver. Try not to look at them." Gretta covered her eyes.

"It's not that bad," Morgan whispered.

"It is. How would you like to see a board with a bunch of dead dogs and cats stuck to it?"

"Ugh. That's horrible." Morgan tried not to gag.

"Well, there you go."

"Shh," Morgan whispered. "People are looking at me. Be quiet."

Julie turned around in her seat. "Did you say something?" she asked.

"No, I was, uh, just reading over the homework." Morgan shuffled the papers on her desk and pretended to study them.

Mrs. Grossinger called the class to attention and began to take roll.

"That woman is evil," Gretta whispered. "I can see it in her aura."

"She's mean, that's for sure," Morgan said.

Gretta was quiet for the next few minutes while the class went over their homework, but soon she was talking again. "Is this class almost over? Zeus, I've never been so bored in my whole life."

"We've only been here ten minutes. We have forty to go," Morgan whispered to her.

"Forty more minutes? Crickets, I'd rather drink hemlock. I may have to do something about this."

"Gretta? What do you mean?"

Gretta shrugged. "Oh, nothing. Don't get your wings in a flap."

"Gretta?" But the fairy had disappeared.

A few minutes later, while Mrs. Grossinger was writing on the blackboard, a large drop of water splashed on her head. She put her hand up to brush it off when another and then another fell on her. She stared up at the ceiling. "Now what? Don't tell me the roof is leaking.

Has it started raining?" She looked out the window. The sun was shining, and there wasn't a cloud in the sky. Several more big drops fell on her.

"Whoever has the squirt gun had better hand it over now, or that person will sorely regret their little game." Mrs. Grossinger stalked up and down the rows of desks, looking for the culprit. More drops fell on her, splattering on her head and shoulders and dripping down her forehead into her eyes. "This is outrageous. When I find out who is responsible for this . . ." She grabbed a wad of tissues from the box on her desk and dried her face; but the drops kept falling, faster now, and bigger.

Kids were beginning to laugh. Brushing water out of her eyes, Mrs. Grossinger went to the closet, took out an umbrella, and raised it. "I don't know what's going on here, but I assure you I will get to the bottom of this. Meanwhile, a little rain never hurt anyone. Everyone take out a piece of paper. We'll have a quiz."

That was when the wind began to blow. It whistled through the classroom, riffling papers and hitting Mrs. Grossinger with such force that the umbrella was blown inside out.

"You, Jeremy. Close those windows," Mrs. Grossinger shouted above the noise of the wind.

"The windows *are* closed, ma'am," Jeremy told her.

The wind blew a book off the desk, and it dropped onto Mrs. Grossinger's foot.

"Ow," she shouted. She collapsed into her desk chair, looking close to tears.

She cleared her throat and straightened her suit. "It appears that we have a problem with the air-conditioning system in this room. I am going to get Maintenance. Class dismissed."

Chapter Nine

As the students were gathering up their books and leaving the classroom, Gretta appeared again on Morgan's shoulder.

"I can't believe you did that!" Morgan whispered.

Gretta giggled. "Why not? It didn't hurt anything, and it got us out of this horrible class. Let's go. I can't stand being in this room another second."

"We have to go to study hall now. They won't let us just hang out, you know."

"Study hall? What's that?"

"It's a place you go when you don't have a class. You're supposed to do your homework."

"Sounds boring," she said with a yawn. "How about we go across the street to that café I noticed this morning? I'm hungry."

"Gretta, this is school. They don't let you just come and go whenever you want. We can't leave till the end of the day."

"Juniper. Sounds more like jail than school. And I thought FGTA was bad."

They were on their way to Morgan's locker when they turned the corner and saw Ben and Sam coming down the hall. "That's him," Morgan whispered to Gretta. Quickly, before they saw her, Morgan ran around the other side of the block of lockers. Ben and Sam stopped at Ben's locker. "Quick. Do it now," Morgan whispered.

"I see what you mean. He is cute," Gretta said.

"Hurry up. Here comes Mrs. Grossinger. She'll ruin everything."

Gretta whispered the incantation and pointed her wand. "Okay. Say his name," she whispered.

Morgan stepped out from behind the lockers. "Hi Ben," she said. At the exact same moment, Mrs. Grossinger came marching down the hall and roared, "Sam Leighton! I need your permission slip for tomorrow's field trip. Have it in my office by this afternoon. As for the rest of you, why are you here and not on your way to class?" She went past them and turned the corner to go to her office. Sam dropped his backpack by Morgan and followed Mrs. Grossinger.

Ben looked at Morgan. "Hi. How are you feeling?"

"All better." Morgan smiled.

"Uh-oh," Morgan heard Gretta whisper. Now what? she wondered. Everything seemed fine. She wasn't sneezing, she wasn't turning blue, and Ben seemed to want to talk to her.

"That's good," Ben said. "How'd your protest turn out? I thought it was cool."

"Thanks," Morgan said. "It was okay."

"Look, if you need help making up that computer lab you missed, I could help. I mean, we are partners."

"Really?" Morgan's heart skipped. "That'd be cool."

Ben smiled at her. "Sure. Well, see you."

Ben went down the hall toward his class, and Morgan, dazed with happiness, whispered to Gretta, "It worked. No sneezing. And whatever you did to him, it worked. Oh, thank you, Gretta."

"But I—," Gretta began.

"Wait. Shh. Here comes Sam," Morgan said.

Sam came back and picked up his backpack.

"Sam, guess what!" Morgan was about to tell him about her conversation with Ben, but his eyes were glazed over and a goofy smile was stuck on his face. "Sam? What's wrong? You look kind of funny."

"Nothing. Nothing's wrong." Sam's smile grew wider. "It's just, did you ever notice how . . . attractive Mrs. Grossinger is?"

"Mrs. Grossinger?" Morgan laughed. "That's not even funny, Sam. That's sick."

"No, I mean it. Her face, it's so strong and yet, kind of gentle, too." Sam gazed down the hall toward Mrs. Grossinger's classroom.

Morgan's jaw dropped. "Sam, you're scaring me. You are joking, aren't you?"

The bell rang, and Sam wandered off slowly down the hall.

Morgan stared after him. "Gretta?" she whispered. "Gretta! What have you done to Sam?"

Chapter Ten

"Oops," said Gretta.

"What do you mean, oops?" Morgan demanded.

"I guess I kind of got the wrong guy. I thought Sam was Ben. It's your fault really. You didn't tell me which was which. How was I supposed to know?"

"You thought Sam was Ben? You put a love charm on Sam?" Morgan cried.

"Right. And that teacher was the first to say his name, which means—"

"Sam's in love with Mrs. Grossinger?" Morgan finished.

"Right again."

"This is awful." Morgan slumped against her locker. "We've got to get this spell off Sam before he makes a total fool of himself. If anyone else finds out he's got a crush on Grossinger, he'll never be able to show his face in this school again." She grabbed her backpack and started down the hall to her English class. "The minute we see Sam you take that spell off him," she told Gretta.

"Um, it might not be so easy," Gretta muttered.

"What do you mean, not so easy?" Morgan asked.

"See, it's a naming spell. Which means that the person who said his name has to unsay it," Gretta explained.

"But that's Mrs. Grossinger. And she doesn't know anything about the spell. And we can't tell her, obviously," Morgan said.

"I know. That's the problem," Gretta said.

Morgan realized that people were staring at her. She looked as if she were talking to herself.

There were still a few minutes left before class, so she slipped into the girls' restroom. Luckily it was empty.

"Look, Gretta. You better come up with something. We can't have Sam going around mooning over Mrs. Grossinger. We just can't."

"Well, I'll have to get my fairy arts manual. And I'll have to call Tuti." Gretta flew in frantic circles around the restroom.

"Great. Do it," Morgan said.

Morgan didn't see Sam again until lunch period. As they walked together to the cafeteria, he said, "Let me ask you something. Do you think it would be weird for a kid to ask a teacher to the Mid-Semester Dance?"

"Are you kidding? Not only would it be weird, it's probably illegal or something," Morgan told him. This was even worse than she thought.

"Oh." Sam sighed.

"Who did you have in mind?" Morgan asked.

"Mrs. Grossinger. Who else?"

"Sam, this thing with Mrs. Grossinger. I know you can't help the way you feel, but I really think you should keep it to yourself."

"Yeah, you're right. I don't want anyone else to get ideas. When they realize how incredible she is, they'll start to feel the same way," Sam said.

Gretta was riding on Morgan's shoulder, and she whispered, "Don't worry. I've got a plan."

Morgan ducked into the girls' restroom. "Okay. What's the plan? It better be good. Some fairy godmother you're going to make. Ever since you came it's been one disaster after another."

"Look, this is as much your mistake as it is mine." Gretta glared at her. "How was I supposed to know that Sam wasn't Ben?"

"You could have asked before putting one of your stupid spells on him. And it would have to be the only time you got it right."

Gretta frowned and beat her wings so furiously they buzzed. "If you feel that way, then I'm going home. You can fix this yourself." With that she disappeared.

"Gretta, wait. . . ."

But the fairy was gone. Morgan dashed out of the restroom.

"Gretta! Gretta wait, I'm sorry," Morgan called.

"Hi Morgan." It was Ben. He looked around, puzzled. There was no one else in the hall.

"Umm, hi Ben." Morgan's face burned.

"Are you practicing for a play or something?" he asked. "Who are you talking to?"

"Yes, a play. That's right," she said. "Gretta, Gretta, I'm sorry. Don't go," Morgan called. She raced down the hall, leaving Ben staring after her.

Chapter Eleven

After school Morgan called Hattie in from the backyard and raced upstairs to her room.

"Gretta? Look, I'm sorry, but I've got to talk to you. Gretta?" Morgan peeked into the dollhouse. Gretta was sitting at her desk writing.

She glanced up at Morgan and then went back to her writing.

"Gretta, please. I didn't mean to yell at you. I was just upset about Sam and everything."

"Hummph," Gretta said without looking up.

"Gretta, listen. I'm really really sorry. I know you're doing the best you can. Please talk to me."

Oliver blinked rapidly off and on as he hovered over Gretta's desk. Gretta said, "Don't pay any attention to her, Oliver. She doesn't need us. She thinks it's easy being a fairy godmother."

"No, I don't think that at all," Morgan said. "It wasn't your fault mixing up Sam and Ben. It could have happened to anyone. It was my fault. You're right about that. I should have—"

"Okay, okay. I forgive you," Gretta said. She put down her pen and came and sat on the steps of the dollhouse.

"Oh, thank you." Morgan let out a sigh of relief. "I was so worried when you disappeared."

"I just came back here. I'm trying to get caught up on my studies. I'm really behind what with all this spell-making."

"I know. I'm sorry. Did you get caught up at all?"

"Actually, I didn't get much chance. I had just sat down at my desk when I heard your father. He scared the crown off me."

"My father? What was he doing home in the afternoon?"

"He was with that Louise Bentley. He was showing her the house. They were talking about fixing it up," Gretta told her.

"What?" Morgan cried.

Gretta nodded. "Louise said the house was darling. All it needs is a little paint and polish."

"Are you sure you weren't dreaming?" Morgan asked.

Gretta laughed at her. "If I were dreaming it wouldn't be about your father and Ms. Bentley, you can bet your wand on that. By the way, your dad left you a note in the kitchen. Did you see it? Something about going shopping this afternoon."

Morgan found her dad's note on the message board in the kitchen. *Morgs—I'll be home early today so we can go shopping. See you around 4:00.*

It was almost four now. Morgan ran back upstairs to get ready.

"Just let me finish polishing my wings," Gretta said. "I haven't been shopping in forever!"

Morgan froze. "You're coming?"

"Of course. I have excellent taste in clothes. You'll need my help."

"Oh. Well, okay. But—"

"Don't worry. I'll just ride on your shoulder. I'll be as quiet as a caterpillar."

Morgan heard her father's car pull up, and in a minute he called, "Morgs? You ready for our shopping spree?"

"Look, Gretta. Just remember I can't talk to you," Morgan whispered as Gretta landed on her shoulder.

In the front seat of the car, Morgan found a stack of her magazines. "Why are these here, Dad?"

"I've been looking through them for dresses for you. I wanted to be up on the latest fashions," he said. "Where shall we go first?"

"Let's try Les Belles," Morgan said. "Ellen and I saw some cute dresses there on Saturday."

"Les Belles it is," he said.

In the shop Morgan tried on several of the dresses she had seen with Ellen, but none of them looked right. "That one's cute," Gretta said, "but you need something with more zing."

"How about this one, Morgs?" her father asked. He held up a hideous purple dress that

looked like something Morgan's grandmother would wear. Gretta burst into laughter. "Your father's a riot."

"He's serious," Morgan whispered. "I don't think so, Dad."

His smile fell. "But there was one just like it in *Today's Fashions.*"

"It's just not me," Morgan said.

A few minutes later Morgan stood in front of the mirror in the dressing room at Evenings, fighting back tears. This was a lost cause. The minute they had walked into the store, a heavy-set middle-aged woman with helmetlike hair and lots of makeup had swooped down on them.

"My name is Delores. What can I help you with?"

Morgan explained about the dance and dress, and Delores said, "Well, you've come to the right place. Dad, you just sit right here and make yourself comfortable." Morgan's father sat obediently on the bench. "I'm going to find this little lady the perfect dress." Delores herded Morgan into the dressing room and returned a minute later with an armload of dresses.

"Try this one," Delores commanded. "It's gorgeous."

Morgan put the dress on. It was a shiny pea green brocade with layers of dark green tulle tacked on around the hips.

"Ugh!" Gretta cried. "Take it off. That dress looks like moldy lettuce. You could do better at a grocery store."

"Beautiful," Delores said, closing a hook in the back.

"It's not really me," Morgan said. "I was looking for something a little more, I don't know, casual."

"Casual. I thought you said it was a dance you were going to," Delores said.

"Shall I turn her into a mouse?" Gretta asked.

"No!" Morgan shouted.

"No?" Delores said. "But you said—"

"No, I mean, it *is* a dance, but it's kind of a casual dance."

"Well, you look adorable. Come on out and show Dad." Delores dragged Morgan out of the room and shoved her down the hall to where her father was sitting.

"That's a pretty one, Morgs," he said.

"This woman has got to go," Gretta said.

"I know but—," Morgan whispered.

"You see? He loves it," Delores said. "You don't want to let a beautiful dress like this one get away, do you?"

"How about a canary?" Gretta asked.

"No!" Morgan cried.

"I guess that settles it. We'll take it," her father said.

"No, Dad, it's really expensive. I don't—"

"I'm not worried about that. This is a big occasion." Her father beamed.

"Turn around, doll," Delores said. "Let him see it from the back. It has a lovely back." Morgan turned, and while Delores and her father admired her back, she heard a familiar voice. "I thought I might find you two here. Sam said you were going shopping."

"Sally!" Morgan hugged her.

"Oh. Is this your wife?" Delores asked Morgan's dad. Sally said quickly, "No, I'm just a good friend."

"Well, what do you think? We all just love this one," Delores said.

"You do?" Sally asked, leaning toward Morgan.

Morgan caught Sally's eye and gave her head a little shake.

"We do," Delores went on. "Doesn't she look lovely?"

"She does look lovely, but I think the dress is not quite what she's looking for, is it Morg?" Sally asked.

"No," Morgan said gratefully. "It's nice, but it's really not me."

"Well, if this isn't the one, we have several other selections—," Delores began.

Sally cut her off. "Thank you; you're marvelous, but I think we've seen enough." She looked at Morgan for confirmation. Morgan nodded vigorously and made her escape to the changing room.

"It's a good thing Sally came in when she did," Gretta said. "That Delores was about to become a reptile."

"Gretta," Morgan said, but she had to laugh. "She was awful, wasn't she?"

When Morgan came out of the changing room, her father and Sally were standing by the door.

"Delores has got ahold of some other poor customer now. We're free. Thank heavens you rescued us," Morgan told Sally. "Those were the worst dresses."

"They were way too matronly. And that Delores was something," Sally said.

Her father looked confused. "But I thought you liked them," he said to Morgan.

Morgan looked at Sally and rolled her eyes.

Sally just smiled. "Why don't we try Sonya's? Have you been there yet?"

"Sonya's! That's where Ellen got her dress," Morgan said.

"There's a darling one in the window that would be perfect," Sally told her.

At Sonya's they found the perfect dress, a bright peach-colored sundress with satin spaghetti straps.

"It looks like it was made for you. And the color is fabulous with your hair," Sally said.

Her father smiled. "She looks awfully pretty, doesn't she?"

"I love it. It's just what I was looking for," Morgan said.

"Yes," Gretta said when Morgan went back into the dressing room. "It's definitely you. But will it match your crown?"

"My crown? Humans don't wear crowns," Morgan said.

"Not even when you're dressed up?" Gretta asked. "That's the pits."

"Humans are not fairies," Morgan said.

"As if!" Gretta laughed.

As they were leaving the mall, her dad's cell phone rang. "Excuse me," he said, stopping to answer the phone. He turned away, but not before Morgan heard him say, "Hello, Louise."

"Uh-oh," Gretta said. "It's her again."

When her father finished his call, he said, "Listen, something's come up. Sally, would you mind giving Morgan a ride home? I have to meet someone."

"Of course, Jim. She can eat dinner with us, too," Sally said.

As they drove home Morgan said, "Have you noticed that Dad's been acting kind of weird lately?"

"How so?" Sally asked.

"Well, for one thing he's been reading my magazines and giving me fashion tips."

Sally smiled. "Hmm. Fashion tips from a man who thinks a ten-year-old flannel shirt is the ultimate in style. That must be something."

"And he cut out a recipe for making a beauty mask. He wants to help me make it."

"Oh, my." Sally laughed. "But you know, I think it's his way of trying to stay close to you. He knows you're getting older, and he doesn't want to lose you."

"I know. It's kind of sweet really. If only it weren't for that stupid Ms. Bentley."

"Who?" Sally asked.

Morgan frowned. "This woman named Louise Bentley. That's who he was going to meet. I think he might like her."

"What? I mean, I'm just surprised. Very surprised."

"Me too. She's really awful. I can't stand her. I don't know what he sees in her."

"You're sure about this?" Sally asked.

"Yup. They talk on the phone constantly. And earlier today he was showing her all around the house and talking about how they want to remodel."

"Really? He was showing her the house?" Sally sounded as upset by this as Morgan felt.

As they turned onto their street, Sally said, "You'll come for dinner, won't you?"

"Sure."

"What did you say this woman's name was?" Sally asked.

"Louise Bentley," Morgan told her.

"Well, don't you worry. I'll talk to him about this."

Morgan hugged her. "That would be great, Sally. And thanks for your help with the dress. I really love it."

Sally dropped Morgan at her house so that

she could hang up her dress and get some homework to work on with Sam.

"Are you coming to Sam's with me?" Morgan asked Gretta when they were upstairs.

"No, thanks. I've got to talk to Tuti and figure out how to break the naming spell."

"Yes. The sooner the better," Morgan told her.

Chapter Twelve

On Thursday afternoon Morgan went to Sam's house to help him get Marvin ready for the school science fair. All the projects were due by Friday, and the judging would take place next week.

Upstairs Morgan found Sam sitting on the floor of his room with their school yearbook spread open across his knees. "There she is. Look." He held up the book to show Morgan a photo of Mrs. Grossinger. "See what I mean? Look at the smile. It's mysterious. Like that painting everyone's so crazy about. *Moaning Lisa.*"

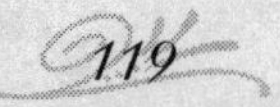

"It's *Mona Lisa.* And I don't want to talk about Mrs. Grossinger."

"Okay. But you have to admit, she really is something," Sam said, smiling dreamily.

Morgan rolled her eyes. "*Sam!* You've got to stop this. You should be focusing on the science fair. How's Marvin?"

Sam sighed.

"He's good. I think he's ready for the fair. Watch this." Sam jumped up and grabbed the control. "Marvin," he commanded, "pick up the book on the floor and bring it to me."

Marvin went over to the yearbook, bent down, and ripped out the page with the picture of Mrs. Grossinger. Before Sam could stop him he had crumpled it up and thrown it into the trash.

"Marvin, no. No. I can't believe you did that. That's the only picture I have of her," Sam shouted.

"Bleep bleep," said Marvin.

"Way to go, Marvin," Morgan said. She tried to give him five but he socked her on the arm instead.

They packed Marvin into a box along with his control and carried it downstairs. Sally was working in the kitchen as usual.

"Well, tomorrow's the big dance, huh?" Sally said.

Morgan nodded. "Yup. By the way, my dad forgot to ask you before if you could give me a ride to the dance. He'll pick Sam and me up afterward."

"Sure. No point in both of us driving both ways."

"Yeah. And my dad has a date," Morgan said.

"He has what?" Sally asked. Her eyes narrowed. She pulled out a sharp knife and put three carrots and an onion on the chopping block.

"A date. With that Louise Bentley," Morgan said with a sigh.

Sally attacked the vegetables. "Are you"—*whack whack thwack*—"sure about this?"

"I heard him on the phone last night telling her he'd meet her at six o'clock tomorrow night."

"I see," Sally said, chopping harder than ever. *Whop whop chop whack.*

"Whoa, Mom. Give those veggies a break. You're turning them into mush," Sam said.

Sally glanced up to see that Sam and Morgan were staring at her. She blushed. "Oh, um, that's what the recipe calls for, honey."

Gretta was waiting for Morgan when she got home.

"Good news," she said. "Tuti can get me the reversal elixir. By tomorrow night Sam's crush on Mrs. Grossinger will be a thing of the past."

"Tomorrow night," Morgan cried. "But that's the dance. Can't you get it any sooner?"

"Tuti can't meet with me until six o'clock tomorrow. She's got classes all day."

"I guess you'll have to bring it to the dance."

"No problem. I planned to come anyway," Gretta said.

"Just make sure you get rid of that spell."

"Trust me. Once I get the elixir nothing could be simpler."

Chapter Thirteen

It was the day of the dance, and Morgan still hadn't asked Ben to go with her. It was too late now; but at least she would see him there, and they could dance together. Just thinking about dancing with him made her heart pound and her knees wobble.

But when Morgan passed Cierra Sinclair on her way to class, she heard her say, "I can't wait till tonight. Ben's picking me up at 7:25 so we can get there right on time."

Morgan's heart sank. Ben was taking Cierra to the dance. She should have known. She had seen them talking together so many times, and

Cierra was so pretty. Of course he would rather go with someone like her.

As soon as she got home, she rushed up to her room and flopped down on her bed. She had kept herself from crying all day, but now she let the tears come.

"Hey. What's wrong? It can't be that bad," Gretta said when she heard Morgan crying. She flew over and sat beside her.

Morgan told her about Ben and Cierra. "Everything's awful. I wish I weren't even going to the stupid dance. And I think Dad is in love with that horrible Louise Bentley. And Sam's in love with Mrs. Grossinger, so I have to go to the dance to get rid of the spell. I wish I'd never heard of love."

"Don't ever say that!" Gretta cried. "Remember what it says in that play you're reading? 'The course of true love never did run smooth.' Even if it was written by a silly human, at least he got that part of it right."

"You're saying William Shakespeare was a silly human?" Morgan asked.

"He sure didn't know much about fairies.

That Puck, honestly. Putting the love potion on the wrong human? You can bet your crown no real fairy would make that kind of mistake."

Morgan snorted.

"What?"

"Nothing," Morgan said quickly. "I guess love isn't running too smoothly for Sam and Mrs. Grossinger."

"That's not love," Gretta said. "That's just a spell."

"So spells aren't real love?"

"Of course not." Gretta went on. "And you just never know what might happen. Maybe things with you and Ben will work out."

"Not a chance," Morgan grumbled.

That night as Morgan and Sam walked toward the gym, she saw Ben and Cierra just ahead of them. Cierra looked gorgeous in a tight red sundress that showed off her figure, flinging her hair around in that way she had. Morgan knew that every boy in the place would be looking at her. She watched sadly as Ben followed Cierra up the steps into the gym.

As soon as Morgan and Sam got inside, Ellen came up to them. "Hi Morg. Hi Sam. Doesn't the gym look great?"

Morgan had to admit it did look good. There were hundreds of balloons and thousands of tiny sparkly lights strung everywhere. "It's like a fairyland," Ellen said.

"Honestly," Gretta snorted. "Shows how much she knows."

"Shh," Morgan whispered, then said, "Your dress is so cool, Ellen. I love it. Doesn't Ellen look great, Sam?"

"Huh?" Sam said. Morgan dug her elbow into Sam.

"Oh, yeah. Great. Really great," he finally mumbled.

But Sam was craning his neck, looking all around the gym. A minute later he spotted Mrs. Grossinger and got that goofy look on his face. "I'll be right back," he said, and wandered off in her direction.

"Sam doesn't seem very happy to see me," Ellen said. "Are you sure he wanted to be my date?"

"Definitely," Morgan said. "I'm positive. It's

just that he, uh, he has to talk to Mrs. Grossinger about something, and he's kind of distracted. He'll be fine."

Morgan hurried after Sam, but he was heading right for Mrs. Grossinger.

"Hi, Mrs. G," he said. "Would you like to dance?"

"Why, Sam, how sweet. I'd be delighted," she said, and Sam took her hand and led her out onto the dance floor.

"You kids don't know this, but I've always loved to dance," Mrs. Grossinger said. Morgan stared in horror as they bobbed and weaved among the dancers. "Gretta," she whispered, "Do something. Break the spell. Now."

"Not now," Gretta hissed.

"Why not?"

"We can't risk it. You've got to get them away from the other kids."

"Look at them. They're not about to quit. Mrs. Grossinger's a dancing queen. Who knew?"

"Well, I can't do a thing as long as they're surrounded by all those other dancers," Gretta told her.

Morgan had an idea. If she couldn't get Sam and Mrs. G off the dance floor, maybe she could get the other kids off. She went over to the disc jockey and asked him to play a salsa. Not many kids would know how to dance to that.

When the salsa music came on, Sam looked disappointed. "I'm sorry, Mrs. G. I don't know how to dance to this kind of music."

"Oh, it's easy. Here let me show you." Mrs. Grossinger grabbed Sam and led him through the steps. The rest of the kids made a circle around them and began to clap as Sam and Mrs. G stomped and spun all over the dance floor.

"Hi, Morgan," a voice behind her said.

Morgan spun around to find Ben smiling at her.

"Hi, Ben," Morgan said, her heart pounding. He looked so handsome in his white shirt and dark blue jacket.

"I've been looking for you," he said.

"You have?" she asked.

"Uh-huh. I, um, thought maybe we could, you know, dance?" Ben blushed.

"You mean, you and me?" Morgan smiled at first, but then she realized what had happened.

Gretta must have put a spell on Ben. That was the only explanation. A few days ago Morgan would have been thrilled if Ben had asked her to dance, or even talked to her. But now she knew it wasn't real. It was just a spell. It was Cierra who Ben really liked, not her.

"I want to dance with you," Morgan told Ben. "I really do. But see, it's all wrong. You think you want to dance with me, but you really don't."

"I don't?"

"No. I'm sorry. It's, oh, I can't explain. I just can't—"

"Morgan, wait. I need to talk to you," Gretta said as she landed back onto Morgan's shoulder.

"Not now," Morgan whispered.

Ben's face fell. "Okay. I'm sorry. I didn't mean to bother you." He backed away and walked slowly out the door of the gym.

"Morgan. I really need to talk to you *now*!" Gretta said.

"What?" Morgan hissed.

"Well, there's a tiny little problem—"

"I'll say," Morgan whispered, watching Sam and Mrs. G surrounded by cheering students. "Just do something. Get this spell off them."

"Don't flip your crown, but I just got a call from Tuti. She forgot to tell me that they have to *drink* the reversal elixir. We can't just sprinkle it over them."

"They have to *drink* it? Can we put it in their punch?"

"Good idea. Get them over to the punch table and I'll put it in their drinks."

Morgan went up to Sam and Mrs Grossinger on the dance floor and said, "Your face is a bit red, Mrs G. Maybe you need a break. May I get you some punch?"

"Thank you, Morgan, but I'm having a wonderful time. I haven't danced this much in years."

"You don't want to overdo it. You might get dehydrated—you always tell us how important it is to drink plenty of fluids when we exercise."

"That's true. Perhaps a short break—"

"That's right. Come on, Sam." Morgan hooked one arm with Sam and one with Mrs. Grossinger and dragged them over to the punch table.

Morgan poured two glasses of punch and Gretta dropped three drops of elixir in each glass. "This punch is delicious. Here, try some," Morgan said.

"Thank you, my dear." Mrs. Grossinger drank hers down and said, "Very unusual."

Sam held his glass out to her. "Would you like another glass, Mrs. G? Have mine if you want."

"*No!*" Morgan shouted. "Uh, I mean, maybe she'd like some water instead?"

"Yes, I've had plenty of punch. You drink that one, Sam."

Finally Sam lifted the glass and drank the punch. He blinked and shook his head, staring at Mrs. Grossinger as if he wasn't sure what she was doing there. Mr. Brooks, the ancient math teacher, held out his arm to Mrs. Grossinger. "What a marvelous dancer you are, Honoria. May I have the next dance?"

"Delighted, Stanley," she said, and they glided out to the dance floor.

"Sam? Are you okay?" Morgan asked.

"I'm fine. It's just, who would have thought Mrs. Grossinger could salsa like that?"

Morgan saw Ellen at the other end of the punch table. "There's Ellen, Sam," she said, giving him a push in her direction. "Don't you want to dance with her?"

Sam headed for Ellen and Morgan breathed a sigh of relief. "Whew. We dodged that bullet, huh, Gretta?" She poured herself a glass of punch and watched Sam and Ellen. They looked like they were having fun. If only she and Ben could be dancing like that.

"Zeus, you look sadder than a broken wand," Gretta said.

"It's just that Ben only wants to dance with me because you put another spell on him. I told you not to do any more. I want him to ask because he really likes me, not just because he's under one of your dumb spells," Morgan whispered.

"But—but I didn't put a spell on Ben. I've been too worried about how to get the spell off Sam," Gretta said.

Morgan slapped her forehead. "You said you didn't put a spell on Ben?"

"Right."

"But he asked me to dance! So that means—"

"That means you should get *your* wings in gear and go, girl!" Gretta told her.

"But what if he's gone back to Cierra?" Morgan moaned.

"Don't just stand there. Go get him." Gretta gave Morgan a shove. "And in the meantime, I'm going to have some fun."

She was watching Cierra, who was flirting with an eighth-grade boy. "That Cierra sure wears her crown high. I may have to teach her a little lesson." Before Morgan could stop her, she flew off again.

Morgan went in search of Ben and finally found him outside the gym, sitting on a bench near the parking lot.

"Ben?" Morgan said.

"Oh. Hi," he mumbled.

"What are you doing out here?" Morgan asked.

"I'm waiting for my mom to pick me up. I'm going home."

"No! I mean, you can't. It's early."

"I guess it's just not as much fun as I thought it would be."

"I'm really sorry about all those things I said before. I really did want to dance with you."

"You did?" Ben looked brighter.

Morgan nodded. "I just wasn't sure if you really wanted to. Wouldn't you rather be dancing with Cierra?"

"Cierra?"

"You brought her to the dance, didn't you? I saw you come in with her."

"Yeah," Ben said. "She lives across the street from us, so my mom told her mom we'd drive her. Actually she's kind of annoying."

"She is?" Morgan couldn't believe what she was hearing.

"Yeah. She always flings her hair in my face," Ben said. "I got a whole mouthful once. I don't like it. Especially in my face." He looked at Morgan. "Your hair's nice though."

"Oh." Morgan blushed.

"So, is now a good time to dance?" Ben asked. "I can still call my mom back and tell her to come later."

"Perfect," Morgan said, taking his hand.

. . .

The disc jockey had just announced that the next song would be the last when Sam and Ellen came up to Morgan and Ben. "Have you seen Marvin?" he asked. "He's gone from the display." The science fair projects were on display in the gym lobby.

"He was there when we came in," Morgan said.

"I know but—" Suddenly there was a commotion on the other side of the gym, and then Marvin zipped by, his lights flashing and his wheels churning. Behind him came Cierra, her arms outstretched toward the robot. "Come back, Marvin. I love you, Marvin. Please come back!"

Just then, Gretta reappeared on Morgan's shoulder. "Cierra will never think of robots in the same way again," she said. "Not too shabby for a fairy godmother in training, right?"

"Right," Morgan whispered.

"Huh?" said Sam and Ben together.

"Night." Morgan smiled. "I said, What a great night."

Chapter Fourteen

The moon was full, and a warm breeze whispered softly through the new spring leaves as Morgan and Ben said good night.

"There's my dad. I guess I'd better go," Morgan said.

"Okay," Ben said, but he kept on holding her hand.

"I'll see you in school on Monday," she said.

"I'll call you tomorrow, okay?" Ben asked.

"Okay."

"Bye."

"Bye."

"See you."

"Call me."

"I will."

"Bye."

"Bye."

"Okay! Enough already. Your dad's waiting." Gretta pushed Morgan toward the car.

Morgan floated down the walk to the car.

"So?" Gretta asked. "I guess the course of love ran smooth enough tonight."

Morgan beamed. "We danced every single dance except the first few."

"See? I knew you and Ben were meant to be."

"It was the best night of my life."

When Morgan got into the car, she noticed that her dad looked sad, not at all his usual cheerful self. He asked how the dance was, but then he just stared at the road and hardly said another word.

"Is something wrong, Dad? You seem kind of down," Morgan said.

"It's nothing for you to worry about, honey. I'm just glad you had a nice time at the dance."

"I did, yes."

He sighed heavily.

"Do you want to talk about it, Dad?"

Her father sighed again. "Well, the truth is, there *was* something I wanted to talk to you about, but things didn't work out the way I had hoped."

"What do you mean, Dad?"

"Well, I had been planning to tell you that I've been seeing, well, that I've been, um—"

"Dating?" Morgan finished for him.

He looked up at her. "You knew?"

"I wasn't sure, but I knew something was going on. And you have been spending a lot of time with her."

He nodded sadly.

"So what happened? You're not dating anymore?" Morgan couldn't help feeling relieved.

"I don't know. She won't even talk to me now. She wouldn't even look at me. She just kept on chopping her vegetables."

"Ch-chopping vegetables?" Morgan asked.

"Yes. Although I really wouldn't call it chopping. It was more like pulverizing." He nodded. "Beating to a pulp actually."

"Wait. I'm confused. Why was she chopping vegetables?"

"I guess she has an event coming up," her father said.

"So Ms. Bentley is a caterer?"

"Ms. Bentley? No. Ms. Bentley is a real estate agent."

Morgan tried again. "Sooo, why was she chopping vegetables?"

"Ms. Bentley wasn't chopping vegetables. *Sally* was chopping vegetables."

Morgan clutched the seat. "Wait, wait, Dad. I don't understand."

Gretta rolled her eyes. "This is exactly how humans get themselves into so much trouble. No communication skills."

"Haven't you been listening, Morgs? I must have done something to upset Sally. Until tonight everything's been so good between us. In fact, we've even been thinking that someday, after we talked to you and Sam, we might get married."

"You and Sally? But what about Ms. Bentley?"

"Ms. Bentley? What about her?"

"But . . . you were going out with her. You had a date. I heard you say you'd see her at six."

"Yes. She was showing me a house. But we were finished by seven, and I went to Sally's to tell her about it. If we do decide to get married, we'll need a bigger house. Louise has shown me several."

"Whoops," Gretta whispered. "Someone messed up big time."

Morgan flopped back onto the seat. As soon as they pulled into their drive, she raced up to her room.

"I don't believe this," Morgan said, collapsing on her bed. "I mean, it's great that my dad's been dating Sally and not Ms. Bentley—"

"You can say that again," Gretta interrupted. She flew to the bed and perched on Morgan's pillow. "Of course, I knew your father was too smart to fall for a troll like Ms. B."

"You knew? Thanks for telling me," Morgan said.

Gretta rolled her eyes. "You humans expect an awful lot. A fairy can only do so much."

"I wish I'd never said anything to Sally. Now she won't even speak to my dad, and it's all my fault."

"It is your fault. And you know what they say."

"What?"

"She who breaks the wand must mend it."

"What does that mean?" Morgan asked.

"It means you better go talk to Sally first thing tomorrow and explain things."

Morgan nodded. For once Gretta was right.

Chapter Fifteen

As soon as she woke up the next morning, Morgan jumped out of bed, leaving Gretta fast asleep in the dollhouse. She dressed quickly and ran out of the house, down the street to the Leightons'. She burst into the kitchen without even knocking. Sally was sitting at the kitchen table drinking coffee. She looked terrible. "Hi, Morg. Sam's still asleep," she said.

"Sally, I've got to talk to you."

"Sure, honey. But if you need advice about something, I'm afraid I won't be much help." As she said it, her eyes filled with tears. "I'm sorry. I'm just a little upset this morning."

"Listen, Sally. Remember what I told you about Louise Bentley and my dad?"

Sally turned away. "Please, Morgan. Don't ever mention that woman's name again."

"But listen. I was wrong. She wasn't dating my dad. She's a real estate agent."

"I don't care what she is. I—what did you say?"

Morgan explained everything. "So you see, he never went on a date with her. I was all wrong about that," she finished.

"So last night he—oh my—" Sally jumped up. "I've got to go," she said and rushed out the door.

Sam was still asleep, so Morgan went back to her own house. She was about to go in the back-door when through the window she saw her dad and Sally sitting at the kitchen table, talking. Her dad was holding both of Sally's hands in his. Instead of interrupting them Morgan sat down on the back steps. Hattie put her head in Morgan's lap. Morgan patted her and whispered, "I think they're making up."

A few minutes later Sally came outside.

“Here she is,” Sally said, sitting down on the steps beside Morgan. “Your dad told you we’ve been . . . well, dating?”

Morgan smiled and nodded. Hattie held her paw up for Sally to hold. “Well, thank you, Hattie,” Sally said, taking Hattie’s paw. “I guess this means we have your blessing.”

Morgan’s dad came outside, carrying two cups of coffee. He handed one to Sally and sat down on the other side of Morgan.

“And how about you, Morg? What do you think of all this?” Sally asked, sipping her coffee.

“I think it’s great. I mean, we’re almost like a family already.”

“We are, aren’t we?” Sally said, putting an arm around Morgan.

“Well, we’re going to take it slowly and give everybody a chance to get used to the idea,” Morgan’s dad said. “What would you think if we all took a vacation together this summer? Maybe rent a cabin on a lake for a few weeks after Sam gets back from his father’s?”

“Cool,” Morgan said. “Can we bring Hattie?”

“Of course,” her dad and Sally said together.

Her dad's cell phone rang. He answered and said, "Why yes, Louise. That sounds fine."

Morgan looked at Sally and rolled her eyes. "It's her," she mouthed.

"See you in a few minutes, then." He hung up and said, "That was Louise Bentley. She has a house to show us. Shall we all go and have a look?"

"I wouldn't mind looking at a house, but why does Ms. Bentley have to show us?" Morgan asked.

"She's a very good real estate agent, Morgs."

"I think we better go along, Morgan," Sally said. "If your dad's taste in houses is anything like his taste in dresses, he might need our input."

Morgan laughed. "Okay. I'll go."

"What's wrong with my taste in dresses?"

"Nothing at all, Jim. We're just teasing you," Sally said, winking at Morgan. She stood up. "I better go see if Sam's up. And I want to talk to him, to explain things."

"I'll call you when Louise gets here."

When she was gone, Morgan said, "Sally's so great."

"She is, isn't she," he said, looking as happy as Morgan had ever seen him look.

He put his arm around Morgan and said, "But you know, sweetie, no matter how much I love Sally, nothing will change the way I feel about you. You'll always be the most important person in my life."

"I know that, Dad. I'm not worried. I think it's great."

From around the corner of the house, they heard, "Yoo-hoo? Anybody home?"

"We're around back, Louise," her dad called.

Ms. Bentley appeared at the back gate. Hattie trotted over to say hello, and Ms. Bentley said, "Oh dear. Perhaps I shouldn't have worn my white pants today."

Morgan's dad stood up. "Put Hatts in the house, please, Morgs."

He went over to the gate. "Come on in, Louise. AHHchoooo!"

"Bless you," said Ms. Bentley. "AHHH-CHOOOO AH-AH-AH-CHOOOO!"

"**AHCHOO!!**" went Morgan's dad.

"**AHCHOO AHCHOO AHCHOO**!!!" went Ms. Bentley.

Morgan was trying not to laugh as she put Hattie inside. Gretta strikes again, she thought.

"Let's—**AHCHOO**—go inside. Maybe it will—**AHCHOO**—be better in there."

"Yes. **AHCHOO**. Must be—**AHCHOO AHCHOO**—allergies."

But inside it was no better. They were in the kitchen sneezing so hard they couldn't talk.

Finally Ms. Bentley said, "I'm going—**AHCHOO**—home to take—**AHCHOO**—an antihistamine. Maybe tomorrow we can—**AHCHOO**."

"**AHCHOO**. Yes. Tomorrow."

Ms. Bentley rushed out, and Morgan's dad came out of the kitchen and said, "The trip to look at the house is off. I don't know what's wrong with me. I can't stop sneezing."

"Maybe you're allergic to Ms. Bentley. That perfume she wears is really strong."

"Don't be silly, Morgan. It's not Louise."

"Well, you've stopped sneezing." Morgan jumped up and ran to her room laughing.

She went right to the dollhouse. "Gretta?" She knocked and then peeked in, but there was no sign of the fairy. And then Morgan saw the note pinned to her pillow. It was written on a small piece of paper about half the size of a dollar bill, and the writing was so tiny Morgan could barely read it.

Dear Morgan,

The BEF found out I've been practicing the arts and called me back to FGTA. I don't think they'll kick me out, but I might be grounded for a while. I don't blame you for this, so don't worry. I liked staying with you and I learned a lot about humans, mainly that they are much nicer than I thought. I'm so glad things worked out with you and Ben.

Sorry I had to leave without saying good-bye. I hope I'll get to come back if I'm not in too much trouble.

Love,

Gretta

P.S. I did a reverse love spell on your dad and Louise Bentley, so I hope that will do the trick. G.

Morgan opened her window and leaned out into the warm spring sunshine. A soft breeze rustled through the leaves, and from somewhere deep in the woods, Morgan heard laughter. "Bye, Gretta," she whispered. "Come back again sometime."

Chapter Sixteen

It had been a great summer, but now it was almost over. Tomorrow was the first day back at school. Morgan was lying on her bed, trying to finish her summer reading, when Hattie went to the window and began to whine.

"What's up, Hatts?" Morgan asked.

From outside the window she heard a familiar voice. "Morgan? Morgan! Get your wings in gear and open the window."

"Gretta?" Morgan jumped up and ran to the window.

"Hurry up. Let me in before the old fruit flies in the BEF change their minds."

Morgan opened the window. "Gretta!" Morgan wanted to hug her but didn't want to squash her, so she held out her hand for Gretta to perch on. "They let you come back?"

"They've given me one more chance to complete my humanstay. I can stay a week."

"A week! That's great."

Gretta flew over to the dollhouse. "Let me put my stuff away, and then we'll catch up."

Morgan lay on her bed on her stomach with her chin propped in her hands, and Gretta sat on the dollhouse steps. Hattie sat down in front of Gretta and gently put her nose out so that Gretta could pat her.

"So, how's Ben?" Gretta asked.

"Ben's great. I didn't get to see him too much this summer because he was away at camp, and I went away with my dad and Sam and Sally. But he called last night, and we talked for an hour. I'm almost looking forward to school because I'll get to see him every day. I'm having lunch with him tomorrow."

"That's great. And how's your dad?"

"He's good. He and Sally are getting married

in October, and we're moving into our new house in time for Christmas."

"So everything worked out fine. I don't know what the BEF were so upset about. Crickets. If it weren't for me, who knows what kind of swamp you'd all be in."

Morgan choked back a laugh. "Well, I'm just glad they let you come back," she said.

"Me too. So, you have school tomorrow, huh?"

"Yeah. And I'm way behind with my summer reading. I still have a whole book to read. I have this English teacher who's known for giving a test on the summer reading on the first day of school. If I don't get going, I'll fail it for sure."

"A test? On the first day of school? She must be a real troll."

"She is."

"Crabgrass. That's no fun. Maybe I should come with you to school tomorrow. If there were a rainstorm in your classroom, she might forget all about the test. Or a snowstorm. That would do it for sure."

Morgan remembered the last time Gretta had come to school. She shook her head. "I don't want to get you in trouble with the BEF."

Gretta waved her hands and whirred her wings. "I'm not worried about them. What they don't know won't tarnish their crowns. Wait a minute." Gretta rummaged in her backpack and pulled out her *Introduction to the Fairy Arts* textbook. She began flipping through it. "Here it is: 'Chapter Six: Spells for Knowledge Enhancement.'"

"But Gretta—"

"Just listen. 'KES number five: Place book under subject's pillow at bedtime. Repeat the following incantation while passing wand over subject's head. Subject must sleep at least six hours to complete knowledge transfer.'"

"What does that mean?" Morgan asked, sitting up.

"It means you just go to sleep; and when you wake up, you'll know everything in the book, just as if you'd read it."

"Wow. But Gretta—"

"You can't waste time studying on my first

night back," Gretta said. "We have a lot of catching up to do. And we have to figure out what you're going to wear tomorrow. You want to look good, don't you?"

"Yeah." Morgan jumped up and went to her closet.

Gretta took Morgan's book and put it under her pillow. "Trust me. This spell is gnome-proof."

Morgan hesitated. "I don't know. . . ."

"I'll bet my wand on it," Gretta said.

"Well," Morgan wavered, "I really don't want to fail that test."

"Of course you don't." Gretta shook her head and smiled. "Silly humans. What would you do without us fairies?"